Chi'Raq Gangstas 2

D1297019

Lock Down Publications and Ca$h
Presents
Chi'Raq Gangstas 2
A Novel by *Romell Tukes*

Lock Down Publications
P.O. Box 944
Stockbridge, Ga 30281
www.lockdownpublications.com

Lock Down Publications
Like our page on Facebook: Lock Down Publications @
www.facebook.com/lockdownpublications.ldp
Cover design and layout by: **Dynasty Cover Me**
Book interior design by: **Shawn Walker**
Edited by: **Lashonda Johnson**

Stay Connected with Us!

Text **LOCKDOWN** to 22828 to stay up-to-date with
new releases, sneak peaks, contests and more…
Thank you!

Submission Guideline.

Submit the first three chapters of your completed manuscript to ldpsubmissions@gmail.com, subject line: Your book's title. The manuscript must be in a .doc file and sent as an attachment. Document should be in Times New Roman, double spaced and in size 12 font. Also, provide your synopsis and full contact information. If sending multiple submissions, they must each be in a separate email.

Have a story but no way to send it electronically? You can still submit to LDP/Ca$h Presents. Send in the first three chapters, written or typed, of your completed manuscript to:

LDP: Submissions Dept
P.O. Box 944
Stockbridge, Ga 30281

DO NOT send original manuscript. Must be a duplicate.

Provide your synopsis and a cover letter containing your full contact information.

Thanks for considering LDP and Ca$h Presents.

Romell Tukes

Prologue

Prior Year

Last year the Chi' Raq Gangsta's had the city of Chicago in a chokehold. When Boss, Malik, and Animal formed a band in Juvenile Detention they had no clue of all the blood they would have to spill to get rich. Boss went from selling pounds of exotic weed to robbing his plug and homie Shooter. Then he started moving weight in Shooter's old hood. Boss paid for his father's appeal lawyer who was serving a life sentence. Now thanks to Boss and his lawyer his appeal motion was granted, and he will be sent back to court for resentencing.

His Uncle Jay helped him on big licks, but Uncle Jay had different plans he was using and setting Boss up the whole time just as he did his brother, Boss' father years ago. When Uncle Jay's main hoe was found murdered, he found out she was an undercover agent. Without hesitation Detective Rodriguez arrested Uncle Jay for a drug charge, then he ratted on Boss and his crew framing them for the undercover cop killing which led to Malik's arrest after Detective Rodriguez's body was found on the shores of a riverbank. Detective Rodriguez's wife Chloe, the beautiful, Spanish woman was having an affair with Animal.

Malik's idea to kidnap Face, a drug lord went all wrong after Face escaped the basement on Animal's watch and ran for his life getting away. When Malik got arrested for the murder of the undercover cop, he was sent to Cook County Jail to await trial. While in the shower Malik's homies stabbed him for killing Shayla but luckily, he was able to come back to life after he died twice.

Lil BD and Jenny became very close and built a strong relationship, they couldn't get enough of each other. Jenny's past relationships were painful. Her recent boyfriend before Lil BD was Pete a basketball player who was fucking her friend Kimmie who had HIV from a kingpin nigga name Loso who was murdered by the Chi'Raq Gangstas.

Pete ended up getting killed by the same crew eventually, but Jenny was focused and happy with her new love life.

Boss' wifey Rosie opened a hair salon and he opened a car lot with a new connect, King Mike, who was Rosie's brother.

Life was great!

Chapter 1

USP Horcelton, West VA

Ty Stone woke up out of his sleep at 5:45 a.m. to the sounds of his alarm clock going off as it did every morning at the same time so he could have thirty minutes to get himself together before the prisoner's doors open.

It was mandatory every morning in Maximum Security prisoners that niggas be up and moving as soon as their cell door opens especially on gang time because shit always popped off in the morning.

Niggas got stabbed in the morning, jumped, race riots broke out, everything you can imagine. Last year Ty saw two G-27 Puerto-Rican gang members from another side of the jail run in their homie's cell and stab him to death.

Ty couldn't wait to get out of prison, he'd won his appeal last year and gave his time back thanks to his son getting him an appeal lawyer who saw loopholes in his case which was able to get him back in court. When he took the old newspapers out of his window to block outside light, he saw a C.O at his door opening it which made him stand because it was too early to open up.

Police brutality in prison was worse than the streets because police would kill a nigga and claim he committed suicide.

"Mr. Johnson—" the old, white racist man asked, looking at a piece of paper, then him.

"Yeah."

"It's yes, boy," the cracker demanded his respect.

Ty laughed at him trying to control his temper, something he'd learned years ago when dealing with guards and inmates. "A'ight."

"Pack your shit up you got an immediate release. I'ma give you ten minutes to pack up and say your goodbyes," the C.O said walking off.

Ty's heart raced and he wanted to jump in the air. He'd been down for twenty-one years straight, he felt as if he was in a dream. Ty brushed his teeth, got dressed, and grabbed some legal work and a stack of mail he tossed in a folder, then left everything else behind food, shoes, clothes, and hygiene products.

"Yo', Pistol, I'm out, Joe," Ty told his homie from Chicago who was a Vice Lord happy to see his man about to touch that free world.

"Don't come back, Joe. I've been down for almost thirty years. You were given a second chance," Pistol said through his door.

Ty nodded in agreement. "Everything in the cell for you and Ed. Love you, Joe, I got all your info, so you already know."

"A'ight take your time and get on your feet first," Pistol told Ty, before going over to his man OG Chuck's cell from Brooklyn, New York who was calling his name because the two had been bidding with each other for years.

"What's up, OG Chuck?"

"Okay, son, I see you. I wish you the best of luck out there, son," OG Chuck said in his old man voice.

"Thank you I hope one day you'll be next," Ty said seriously wishing good men like Chuck and Pistol could see daylight.

"I been locked down thirty years, son. Ru Paul will have a better chance at turning straight before they let me go home, son," OG Chuck said, making him laugh as always.

"No doubt O.G. I'ma keep in touch," Ty said

"I know bro I believe you, son. You been a stand-up nigga since I met you. So, I expect nothing less out of you," OG Chuck said serious.

"Johnson, you wanna go home or cell up with your friends?" a C.O yelled ready to go.

"I'ma take care of that bitch ass C.O. later. Get out of here, kid," OG Chuck said.

As Ty left, inmates were yelling his name and banging on doors showing their respect and love. Ty went to R&D and dressed out of his jail clothes into a designer outfit he didn't even know how to spell called Balenciaga. They dragged him in the bullpen for nearly three hours until 10:00 a.m. because allegedly their computers were down. This was the game Ty was used to now after over twenty years of being caged up like a wild animal.

"You ready, Mr. Johnson?" a tall, white, female C.O. asked, unlocking his cage, handing him his release papers.

"Thank you."

"Sure, come on let me escort you out," she said, he followed her looking at her iron board ass. "So, how long you been in?" she asked as they walked through metal doors.

"Twenty-one years, six months, and eight days."

"Damn, you look like you're only twenty," she said with a chuckle.

"That's what prison does for you when you try to take care of yourself," he said as he waited at the gate for the towers to unlock it.

"I see," she said, opening the gate for him. "Bye," she said.

He walked into the prison parking lot to see his best friend Smitty leaning on a white BMW X5M truck with rims and tint and the morning sun beamed off the paint.

"Welcome home," Smitty said hugging his friend of over thirty years.

Smitty was the same age as Ty and he was under him as a Black P Stone. He was a big man at 6'4 and two-hundred and ninety-five pounds, he was a nightclub security guard and he sold grams of coke to some young wolves from around his way. He'd been there for Ty every step of his bid the whole twenty-one years even with a family and wife that he loved, but he was loyal to Ty and considered him family as well.

"Thanks for coming, big boy, let's get the fuck away from here. These crackers still hanging niggas out here," Ty said climbing in the truck.

"You look young and healthy, Joe," Smitty said checking his friend out seeing that he was fit, had no missing hair, goatee was clean with no gray insight, no rooftop in his head, and all his teeth.

"I wish I could say the same for you," Ty said looking at Smitty's big gray beard.

"If you only knew the half."

"You got everything I asked you for?" Ty asked as the BMW drove down a big deep hill.

"Yeah." He passed Ty a piece of paper with an address on it.

"Thanks."

"Are you sure you want to do this on your first day out?" Smitty asked.

"I have no choice. Bob said today was the day and I knew he would be going there. She is all he knows under his tough skin," Ty said disgusted.

"A'ight. Did you hear what happened to Premium last year? A nigga turned him into mash potatoes outside of his church," Smitty informed.

"I guess God can't save everybody," Ty said remembering when he told Boss his son about how Premium was one of the niggas who ratted on him at trial. Days later, his body was found in his car. It wasn't hard to put two and two together.

"We got a lot of money to get. You still got your old plug? Because the city is open season," Smitty said smiling.

"Yeah, I still got my plug. We're gonna get to it just let me feel shit out."

"Facts," Smitty said, then they talked all the way back to Illinois.

***

Riverdale, IL

Smitty and Ty pulled up to a quiet block to find the address they were looking for which was a two-story house with a two-car garage in the middle of the house dividing it into sections.

"This is it I'll be back. Hold me down," Ty Stone said tucking the pistol Smitty gave him in his lower back.

He made his way to the porch that had two flower-pots full of dead flowers. Ty rang the doorbell twice, then heard a female's voice coming through the door. When the woman opened the door, she was so surprised, it was as if she'd seen Jesus.

"Oh my God, Ty!" Nicole said jumping into her first lover's arms unable to believe that he was out.

Ty didn't tell nobody he'd won his appeal or that he was free today except Smitty and Boss.

"You look amazing," Ty said looking at her thick thighs in her shorts, her big breasts, and her smooth cocoa-brown skin. She looked like Tyra Banks in her prime.

"Come in," she said, letting him inside looking at how sexy he still was, wishing she'd never left him for his brother after she had a baby.

Ty and Nicole had been a thing forever but when he had Boss, she started fucking with Jay his brother and he fell in love with her beauty and pussy. While Ty was lock up, she would write to him and send pics daily when she had time because she worked for a travel agency, so she did a lot of traveling.

"You have a nice place," Ty said sitting in her living room, which was clean, smelling good, and had new tables, carpets, and furniture all over the place.

"Thanks," she said sitting across from him with her legs open showing her stuffed camel toe. "You fresh home, wow. I know you must be horny?" she said, smiling.

Ty knew she was a big ole freak but he'd been gone for a while, so he had to get back in the groove of things.

"Hell yeah."

"Hmmm—your brother should be here later. But until then, how about we catch up?" she said making her way over to him.

She sat in his lap to feel his big dick stabbing her pussy as she got wet. Nicole took off her clothes and his, not trying to waste a second. She loved a fresh home dick it was her best climax. She placed his hard dick into her dripping wet pussy as she bounced up and down slowly trying to feel every inch.

"Ooohhh, yessss, Ty fuck this hairy pussy!" she moaned in pleasure as he licked her big titties flopping up and down like a dolphin fin.

Ty was fucking her so hard Nicole's body started to violently shake as he banged in and out of her.

"Aaahhh, I can't take it, Ty, I'm cumminnnggg!" she screamed cumming hard as her creamy cum came out like a waterfall and she couldn't believe what she'd just experienced.

"Bend over, Nicole," he said.

She hurriedly did as she was told then he rammed his dick in her hairy pussy which was making gushy sounds.

"Give me that dick, Ty! Fuck me harder!" she yelled while he grabbed her thin waist and forced himself in her until no inches were left out. He placed one of her long legs on the couch armrest and went deeper, sliding in her wet tight walls.

"Ooohhh, Ty, ughhhhh I'm cumming again! Don't stop rape me—rape me!" she yelled cumming.

"Shut up," he said, hitting her G-spot hard and harder about to nut in her sweet warm pussy. "Damn, Nicole." He pulled out nutting on her back.

"Oh, hell no, nigga don't waste that!" she yelled turning around trying to catch his thick heavy cum shooting out of the head of his dick.

She took his throbbing dick into her warm mouth and used her thick lips to maneuver up and down on his pole before taking him down her throat. She worked her throat muscles relaxing them so she could let him go deeper as he moaned. She pushed him on the couch and started to go crazy on his dick going faster and faster giving his sloppy neck.

"Fuckkk, Nicoleee—" He gripped her loose wig for support as she slowed down while he face-fucked her in slow motion.

Ty saw a shadow coming inside from the living room window as Nicole was banging the tip of his dick in the back of her throat. Ty saw the enter the house with flowers in his hand and he was at a loss for words.

Ty forced Nicole's head on his dick as she choked and gagged then he jerked and exploded in her mouth making her swallow every drop.

"You taste so good," she said, finally raising her head to see Jay standing there with glossy eyes. "Oh my God, Jay, I'm so sorry it just happened," Nicole said wiping her mouth.

14

Ty got dressed and started laughing as he saw the sick look on his brother's face.

"Good to see you, Jay. The last time I saw you was when you took the stand on me," Ty said.

Nicole covered her big double DD titties with her shirt that had cum stains on it. Ty looked at Jay's hammie down suit and laughed harder.

Jay had no clue that his brother was out of prison. He knew for sure he had a life sentence. He was speechless, scared, heartbroken, and confused.

"I'm sorry, Jay, but we're both older now. You only come see me when your hoes leave you or when you're fucked up. I don't want you no more. Me and Ty gonna work on us, I'm sorry," Nicole said.

Her words cut Jay like a knife in the heart.

Ty looked at her as if she'd lost her mind, then he pulled out his gun and shot her twice in the head causing her body to collapse on her living room oakwood table.

Jay was shocked at what he saw, he didn't even feel the tears running down his face.

"Now that she's out of the way let's have a sit-down or stand up. I waited years for this brother. The day at trial when you smiled and winked at me that vision never left my thought process. Every night you haunted me."

"I'm sorry, Ty, I-I-I-I—" his voice trembled and he was unable to find the right words to use for his disloyalty.

"No justifying, Jay, take your punishment like a man. You was always a pussy. That's why mommy always said she shoulda swallowed you."

"Karma's a bitch," Jay said.

Ty laughed then squeezed the trigger.

Boc! Boc! Boc! Boc! Boc! Boc! Boc! Boc! Boc! Boc!

Ty made sure his brother was dead before walking out.

"You let the whole clip go, nigga?" Smitty said when Ty hoped in the BMW and Smitty raced off.

"I should have," Ty said, feeling no remorse for killing his big brother because he'd been dreaming of this day for years.

"I coulda been taken care of that rat, nigga," Smitty said.

"Nah, I had to do it. He was my blood so I had to do it the right way," he said thinking about how crazy Nicole's head game was but he knew he couldn't leave no witnesses. He refused to go back to prison again because he knew next time it was lights out.

Ty knew Jay was getting out of rehab today from a spot in St. Louis because his man OG Bob was there with him. Bob did time with Ty and saw him grow up. Bob wrote Ty daily, so he kept him posted on Jay. Ty knew Nicole would be the first person that he'd run to because she was his backbone and she never turned her back on him. Because she loved him also but hated when he was on drugs, so they had a distant friendship.

"Where to now?"

"To see my son, then I'm going to my spot you got for me," he told Smitty who'd got him a nice pad in downtown Chi-Town.

Chapter 2

Bogota, Colombia

Animal stood in the barn full of Spanish men dressed in army gear holding assault rifles as they surrounded both of their bosses and watched them torture a man. Animal stood in the shadows off the side, smoking a blunt of some exotic weed he'd found in the city of Bogota. This had been his home for the past year, but he was back and forth from Chicago to Colombia.

He muffled the loud cries of the man being tortured and thought about how fast his life had changed since he came home from prison. Months ago, he and his crew the Chi'Raq Gangstas was kidnapping, robbing, and killing kingpins in Chicago. When he met Chloe he fell in love with her beauty after being shot by Canon one night she saved his life and never questioned his lifestyle.

After he and his crew killed Detective Rodriguez for snooping into their affairs, he found out he was Chloe's husband as they hopped on her private jet. He was shocked she was married but what really confused him was when she thanked him for killing Detective Rodriguez because they were on the verge of divorce anyway. The most shocking news was when she told him she'd been watching him and his crew before they even met, he was lost until she told him the reason why.

Chloe told him she was the boss of a very powerful Colombian Cartel, Crime Family. She told him no because she kept that life from him, so she'd been living a double life for years. He asked her what she wanted with him? Chole explained she wanted to make him a rich and powerful man but it would take time and lots of skills. She wanted him to take over Chicago and the whole Midwest drug trade, he still thought it was a joke.

When Animal got to Chloe's mansion surrounded by armed guards, he didn't know what was going on. She assured him that they were okay, they were there to protect her. He saw everybody treating her as if she was a Queen but when she showed him a basement full of bricks, he knew she was the real deal.

She explained how her whole family was part of the Cartel from her grandparents to her parents and it was in their bloodline. When she was in the states her brother RJ controlled the drug trade and family business in South America.

Malik was locked up and Boss was locking down Chicago's drug trade while they thought he was in Minnesota and St. Louis getting money. Unaware that he was preparing for the major comeback to take over his city's drug trade. Animal walked over toward Chloe and her brother RJ who was standing in front of a young Colombian man in his early twenties with scars and deep knife wounds all over his bloody body.

"Now, Geo, what did you tell the Santos Cartel Family? Because they killed my men and robbed my shipment. You were the only person who knew where the shit was going besides me and RJ," Chloe said dressed in a black YSL satin dress with heels showing a little skin but looking classy at the same time.

"Please, boss, they made me do it. They killed my wife and said my kids were next. I had to give them something," Geo told the truth after hours of torture because he couldn't take the pain no more of being stabbed with icepicks, burned with cigars, and cut open with sharp razor blades.

Chloe looked at her brother RJ who was a spitting image of her, thirty-years-old with a pretty boy swag but he was a vicious murderer.

"I took good care of you, Geo. You was like family to me," RJ said in his heavy Spanish accent.

"RJ, I'm sorry, please don't do this. What would you have done? You're the Godfather to my kids," Geo cried.

"Not no more. Fuck them, bastards. I would've died in honor before I gave my family up." RJ grabbed a gun from one of the guards standing in a circle behind him.

"In the Rabelo Cartel we live by a different set of rules and you know this." Chloe was about done with the whole situation because the truth came out as she suspected.

She'd been going to war with the Santos family for years. Their boss Hector was a snake with a poisonous bite.

RJ looked at Animal standing there, he smiled at the man who he didn't really like at all. He didn't see what his sister saw in him, not to mention he hadn't seen him put in no work yet. "Do us the favor," RJ passed Animal the gun he was holding.

Chloe looked at her brother knowing what he was trying to do. Animal took the gun and shoved it back into RJ's cheek, almost knocking his frail body over in a haystack. Chloe was about to say something until she saw Animal take off his blazer and roll up his sleeves.

Animal grabbed a long sharp razor blade, then made his way over to Geo who was shaking his head no. Animal got behind him and slit his neck with the blade, blood squirted all over Chloe and RJ. Geo's neck hung on his shoulders, Animal cut his tongue out of his mouth with ease, then slowly cut Geo's lips as if he was slicing cheese. Chloe and RJ were at a loss for words they didn't want to see all of this shit as their stomachs started to turn.

Animal was digging the blade into Geo's eyes with force until his eyeballs came out, when he was done Geo looked like a Jeepers Creepers victim. Just when the guards and Chloe thought he was done he cut Geo's chest open and the blade cut into Geo's skin like a knife cutting butter. He dug his bare hand into Geo's chest feeling soft bloody tissue and organs searching for his heart.

Two of the guards vomited in a pig cage, they couldn't watch the scene anymore because it was extreme, they were used to beating niggas to death and shooting their victims but never had they seen some Hannibal shit like this.

Once Animal got to Geo's heart, he snatched it out, long bloody cards and strings were attached to it. He walked over to RJ and placed everything in his hands. RJ quickly dropped it disgusted, Animal got his blazer and walked out.

"That's what you get. I told you about that shit, stop being so racist. It's not the time or place," Chloe chastised her brother to his face before chasing her man.

RJ was pissed that Animal had done his best friend like that. *He could've just shot him and been done with it.*

"DeWayne," Chloe said as Animal walked back to the mansion on the 13-acre land with a small farm full of banana trees, cocoa beans, vegetables, and oilseeds.

"What? I gotta get ready to head back to the states," he said, stopping as Chloe walked up on him, feeling the warm, tropical wind blowing her long, dirty blonde hair.

"I'm sorry about that back there. But you took that a little far, baby," she said holding his hand and walking with him down a road leading to the back of their 23,214 square foot palace.

"My name is Animal for a reason. I don't have time to prove shit to nobody. Not you or your brother!"

"I know, babe, but you don't have to prove nothing to me. I love you and that's that. Now can we go inside so I can get some dick? You just made me so horny back there, Papi," Chloe said.

"Oh, yeah, how horny?" he said sliding a finger under her dress, into her wet dripping pussy, her juices rolled down his finger.

The two went upstairs and fucked for three hours before he took her private jet to Chi-Town, to meet up with Boss.

Chapter 3

Cook County Jail, Chi-Town

"It's on you, Ra Ra," Malik told his celly who was looking into his hand to see what card to throw out next as he, Malik, and two other inmates played a game of spades.

"God damn, nigga, you play like my grandma," Sub G said sitting at the table across from Ra Ra.

"I'm trying to play in your grand mom's pussy, nigga. What the fuck you talking about?" Ra Ra said, throwing out an Ace of spade cutting diamonds as he took the cards.

"Good move, Joe," Malik said, hoping he won because there was $50 in commissary on this game and a couple of sticks of weed rolled up in tissue wrapper.

Ra Ra threw out a king of diamonds as Sub G and his partner looked at Ra Ra. Even Malik looked because he'd just cut diamonds with a spade as if he didn't have any more diamonds.

"Nigga you just cut diamonds you can't do that," Sub G a Gangsta Disciple from Chicago Heights said getting upset.

"I ain't cut shit this the last hand. Play the shit out and stop crying like a bitch," Ra Ra said as Sub G's partner threw out a card wanting no problems with the nigga Ra Ra who he knew from the streets and he was nothing to fuck with.

"Man, this ain't right," Sub G said

"Sub G play your card," Ra Ra said calmly

"I quit, Joe, I'm good," Sub G said and Malik laughed.

"So, pay up, nigga," Ra Ra said placing his cards on the table taking his quitting as a win.

"I'm not paying you, bro, you just cheated. Come on, Ra Ra, that's not right," Sub G said trying his best to hide how scared he was. Sub G was a big, fat, black nigga who was in jail awaiting trial for killing one of his workers for stealing from him.

Ra Ra quickly pulled out a knife so long it was half his size with an ice pick point. When Sub G's partner saw this he got up and did what he knew best, ran to his cell.

Malik just sat there in the last year and some months he'd seen his celly stab four niggas and one almost died.

"You not going to what?" Ra Ra walked across the table as Sub G walked the opposite way trying to get away from the biggest knife he'd ever seen.

"I'ma pay you, right now, bro," Sub G said.

All the inmates in the dayroom were ready to look in because everybody knew how Ra Ra got busy with a knife.

"You want to play Rummy 500?" Ra Ra said sitting down tucking his knife in his shorts that he normally wore under his jail jumpsuit. Ra Ra watched Sub G go to his cell and get his commissary ready.

"Hell nah, I ain't playing cards with your dumb ass. You can't be doing shit like that, bro. What if he comes back and blows your ass up," Malik said looking at his celly who was a live wire.

"I'll kill that nigga in this bitch," Ra Ra stated.

Sub G came back to the table with a bag of food and ten sticks of weed. "Here's everything, I even put six flat book forever stamps in there. So, we good, right Ra Ra?" Sub G asked with fear on his face as his lips trembled.

"We good, bro. How about another game?" Ra Ra smiled as Malik gave him an evil look.

"Maybe another day, I'ma little tired," he said walking off.

Malik shook his head. Ra Ra was a nineteen-year-old Vice Lord from Ingleside. He was locked up for two homicides, he'd just beaten six months ago but he had six more months to do for a probation violation.

Malik walked back to his cell to do some reading by one of his favorite authors, *Romell Tukes A Gangsta Qu'ran* was one of his favorite books. Last year Malik almost lost his life after being stabbed multiple times in the shower by his own Vice Lord homies. Shayla's cousin put a hit out on Malik for the death of Shayla and Dirt. Two weeks after Malik was stabbed, Boss found out and Shayla's cousin who put a hit out for Malik and the Chi Raq Gangstas was found dead in the trunk of his car.

When niggas in the jail found out Malik was one of the Chi' Raq Gangstas they treated him like royalty. The crew's name was the biggest in Chicago but nobody knew who the mysterious gangstas were.

Malik's celly wanted to be down so bad with the Chi Raq Gangstas that was all he talked about. Malik knew Ra Ra was a standup nigga, so he promised Ra Ra when he got out, he would hook him up with Boss.

Boss had been holding Malik down 100%, as well as Simone. He wanted for nothing, plus, he still had a big bag in the streets. Boss was holding down his traps and opening shops all around the city. His name was ringing in the jails but nobody had a clue he was a Chi Raq Gangsta.

Malik hadn't heard from Animal since he'd been locked up, but the two never saw eye to eye anyway.

His case was big, killing a cop was like killing the pope in the city. Trial was set up for a few months, he had faith and so did his lawyer, but he knew the DA wanted a conviction somehow. The DA was also trying to pin Detective Rodriguez's murder on him charging him with *Conspiracy to murder an officer*. Malik pulled out a stick of weed and made a fire with two AA batteries and smoked himself to sleep trying to picture the streets.

***

Chicago Heights

Boss was in his house getting dressed so he could go meet with Animal who was back in town. A couple of months ago, Boss and Rosie bought a nice two-story home in the suburbs of Chicago Heights to get away from the hood. The house was beautiful with four bedrooms, three and a half baths, a newly remodeled kitchen, a spacey living room, a dining room area, walk-in his/her closets, central air, granite countertops, Baldwin Bronze hardwood floors, and designer furniture and drapes.

Boss wore a pair of Gucci shorts, a Gucci T-shirt, Gucci Loafers, and a curb link diamond bracelet to match his Cuban Link 6.6 carats with 19k white gold in his necklace.

Life was good, Boss had a car lot and Rosie had a hair salon in Downtown, Chicago which was a hot spot for the upper and lower class. He had the streets on lock he was supplying Chicago Heights and most of the towns on the outskirts of Chi-Town. His connect King Mike was blessing him with pounds of coke because he moved work like a bodybuilder.

The other day he spent the whole day with his pops who was fresh home and doing good for himself. Ty already had a nice condo, the latest designer clothes, jewelry, and a fresh pearl white Mercedes AMG CLA 45.

Boss wished Malik was home to enjoy the wealth and success they got out of the mud, but jail was part of the game. He was going to ride with Malik until the end no matter how much time he got because he held his water like a true G unlike niggas nowadays in the streets.

Boss saw that he had a missed call from his two workers who were moving work for him. He had to re-up because he was down to his last ten keys and that wasn't near enough. He sent King Mike a text letting him know he needed to see him. Since Malik got locked up, he gave up robbing because he didn't need to anymore. He was up and Chi Raq Gangstas was a household name in the city.

Word was the whole city wanted his crew dead, niggas had thousands on the crew's heads because they'd killed a lot of powerful gang leaders and kingpins around the city. Boss walked outside to feel the nice summer heat, it was a perfect day to go to a beach. He hopped in his new, all-black Rolls Royce Wraith Black Badge Edition with the stars in the ceiling.

***

Downtown, Chi-Town

Rosie's Salon was packed today with customers from all races and ages getting ready for the 4th of July weekend. The salon was large with two different sections, ten stylists who were the best in the city, white marble floors, a mirrored ceiling, a state-of-the-art surround sound system, eight 52-inch flat-screen TVs for the guests, and male bartenders serving drinks to the women. Rosie was in her office writing checks to cover the monthly bills for the salon, then she had to sign off on all her employee's checks. She wore an all-white Chanel, two-piece suit with white Chanel heels to match. She was still beautiful with her Spanish features that made men do double-takes and since she'd been in the gym her ass was bigger thanks to squats.

Her love life with Boss was wonderful. The only thing they were missing was a family because they were married, now she was ready for the icing on the cake.

Rosie's assistant manager came into her office with a crazy look on her face as Rosie heard yelling and cursing coming from out front.

"This new bitch, Tamika, just pulled a big ass patch out of her client's. The client is going ham," Julia said in her Dominican accent, dressed like a hooker in her tiny skirt, showing her long legs.

"Shit, okay." Rosie got up.

There was always something going on from fistfights, arguing, pepper spraying, and even tug team fights. Rosie saw it all in her shop. She had something to tell Boss every night and he couldn't believe it.

Romell Tukes

Chapter 4

University of Chicago

This was Jenny's last year of college, she was striving to obtain her nursing degree. Being the first person in her family to go to college was the best feeling even though her mom Ashley had a good, state job working as a social worker for Cook County. After class Jenny made her way to the student hall build where most students went to study and she had a lot of that to do. It was so hot outside she regretted wearing an Adidas tracksuit with long sleeves.

"Yo,' Jenny, what's up, beautiful? When can a nigga get a second of your time?" a tall, light-skinned basketball player said following her as she stopped.

"Nigga, never, you broke and you fuck with basic bitches. So, that makes you a basic ass nigga," Jenny said walking off leaving him standing there pissed off because he'd never got played by no bitch like that.

Jenny made it in the student hall build and went on the second floor to study. Niggas eyed her sexually, she brushed it off and focused on her up and coming exams. Jenny's love life had been amazing. She and Lil' BD was living their best life and enjoying trips to Miami, Atlanta, New York, and Paris.

Jenny was now a high-ranking member of the BDs. She was the Godmother and Lil BD was the big homie in the streets. He took over Loso's position who was killed by the Chi' Raq Gangstas.

For Christmas Lil BD bought her an all-black Porsche Cayenne Turbo truck with rims and tints, black and red two-tone interior leather seats.

She knew her boo was still in the streets, but she was just glad he wasn't killing niggas because last year he and Hitler were turned up drilling shit all across the city.

Lil BD planned to open a sneaker store in North Riverdale Mall next month. She was glad he was thinking outside the box and cleaning his money.

"Hey, Jenny, gurl I see you're doing the same thing I'm doing," her classmate Heidi said as she sat at the table with Jenny, unpacking her textbooks and laptop.

Heidi was a pretty snow bunny who looked like a Barbie doll but thick with a body of a ghetto black girl.

"I'm glad you're here, I need some help on this Sarcoplasmic Reticulum shit. I know it helps release calcium into the body, but what else?" Jenny asked Heidi who was a borderline genius.

"Well, as calcium is released during contraction then binds to troponin and changes the position of tropomyosin-troponin on the action filament," Heidi said as if it was fresh on her thoughts.

"Okay, so that allows the myosin to bind with the actin filaments," Jenny said and it started to make sense.

"Yeah, gurl you got it. Oh, I just saw that tall, light-skinned basketball player with the green eyes. He's talking about when he makes it to the NBA, he wants me to be his Kim K," Heidi said laughing at how corny he was.

"He just tried his hand with me." Jenny shook her head.

"I prefer dark chocolate, big muscles, and some jail tattoos," Heidi said, making Jenny laugh, then they got back to studying.

Jenny and Heidi ended up going out to eat at a local grill & chicken restaurant near the college campus.

***

Buff City

Lil BD and Hitler were both posted up on their cars parked next to each other. Lil BD had an all-white BMWi8 and Hitler had a sky-blue Audi RS7. The two had the drug game on lock in Buff City from 100 Street to 119th Street, they had every type of drug except coke, crack, and dope. Both men knew selling coke or dope was the fastest way to a prison cell.

"You holler at Ralley and them niggas?" Lil BD asked Hitler who was drinking from a foam cup full of thick lean.

"Yeah, he's talking about some GDs robbed his spot the other night. Shit, I told that nigga, I don't give a fuck if Bruh Man from the fifth floor came through his window. He better have that bread," Hitler said seriously referring to his little homie.

"A'ight, bro, I'm about to shoot across town," Lil BD said looking down the block to see over sixty young BDs selling work, chilling, and enjoying the summer waiting for some beef or ops to slide thru.

Lil BD made sure their guys had poles, with more drums than the movie drumline. Guns and assault rifles were everywhere in alleys, in garbage cans on the side of buildings, under cars, and on persons.

"Hit me later, I'ma be out here with the guys. Then I gotta go holler the 4s," Hitler said with a slur in his voice taking a big sip of lean as some spilled on his Dior shirt.

"Some niggas don't need to wear designer, bro," Lil BD said, watching Hitler brushing his red stain into his $2500 Dior T-shirt.

As Lil BD pulled off, he noticed a text from Jenny.

//: Wyd?

He texted back. *//: Driving.*

He figured she was home it was close to 8:00 p.m. normally she would come home at 6-7 p.m. she was a full-time student so she would have evening and night classes.

Since he'd been getting money, he'd been moving differently because he had too much to lose. He was feeling most of the BDs in Buff City niggas needed him. When one of the original BD members heard what Lil BD was doing for the guys he gave him and Jenny a lot of status while he was in the feds serving a life sentence.

Lil BD hadn't seen his brother in months and he was with that because they never really had a real relationship except as kids but they were grown now.

Lil BD disliked his brother's Boss because he always felt as if he was trying to belittle him or treat him like a little nigga. Their man always felt the tension and she tried to explain that no matter what they were blood and one day they would need each other.

Lately, he'd been hearing Boss had the city on lock with the keys. Lil BD wasn't mad he was proud his bro was on top of his game but that didn't change how he felt about him. Since his sneaker store was scheduled to open soon and his guys were on their way up, he was satisfied. He wasn't a greedy nigga like most niggas. He saw greed being a real nigga's downfall, so he focused on just maintaining and saving for a rainy day.

The BMWi8 Coupe flew down the city's dark streets, blasting the artist *A Boogie Wit da Hoodie* new album. He sang to the song on his way to meet with a new molly plug a nigga named Smitty.

***

Detroit, Michigan

Face and B. Stone were in a well-known strip club called Ace of Spades, watching strippers slid up and down poles on stages as the City Girls blasted through the club speakers.

The two men were in their VIP section drinking Deuces out of the bottle while enjoying the beautiful women making a living. Face and B. Stone had been hiding out in Detroit getting a bag. They had a crew on the Westside of town moving weight for them. They also had a team in 6 mile and 7-mile clocking in big money.

After being kidnapped by the Chi Raq Gangstas, Face was able to get away alive luckily, and he knew he had to relocate before they were to come back. Even with B. Stone killing Malik's mom and stepdad that did nothing for Face and he knew Boss and Animal were still out there. Face would never forget any of their faces because they haunted his dreams every night.

Recently B. Stone had gotten word that a nigga name Boss had the city on lock with the bricks and was doing big things. Face and B. Stone were planning a major comeback soon. He planned to kill all three men with a slow death.

"You ready, Face? I ain't feeling this shit tonight, I already tricked off twenty-five gees," B. Stone said as he watched a thick, short-haired chick coming toward their VIP section.

"Yeah, we going to the hotel I was just waiting on her," Face said as the super, thick and juicy Dej Loaf look-alike approached the VIP in a pair of thongs with no bra. Her small breasts jiggled with every move and her thong was splitting her thin pussy lips apart. Face stared at the tattoos all over her body feeling his dick grow in his Versace jeans.

"I'm coming with you tonight, daddy," Tatted up Lust said to Face sitting on his lap letting her ass cheeks hang off his legs.

"That depends," Face said

"On what, daddy?"

"How good your pussy is," Face said sliding two fingers into her warm wetness.

"Mmmmm!" she moaned.

"You ready?" Face asked smelling his fingers to smell the scent of light musk, but it wasn't too bad he could work with it.

***

In the hotel, room Face had her thick legs in the air as he dug deep into her walls driving her crazy as her sexual urges rose and she submitted herself.

"Uggghhhh!" she moaned wanting to shout his name, but she didn't know it. "Jesus—ohhhh, fuckkk!" she yelled as his dick pushed in and out of her tight pussy. After four kids she still had the snapback pussy that made niggas go crazy.

When he nutted in her she'd already climaxed three times to his one due to the molly she'd popped before she left the club which had her on a different planet.

Face bent her over, making her grab her ankles as he slapped her big ass, he could tell it was fake, but it looked real. His dick was ripping her womb apart and she loved the pain from his massive dick. She felt it in her kidneys almost puncturing her lungs.

"Ooohhh my God, bab." He spread her ass cheeks wider as her pussy walls squeezed tightly around his dick.

His pelvis was pressed on her ass cheeks and she took every inch trying to back her ass up, but he was pounding her out too hard.

Her body almost flew into the hotel dresser because he was fucking her so hard. Then suddenly he started smelling a strong odor coming from her pussy.

"I'm cummingggg—ugghhh yesssss!" she yelled cumming hard feeling dizzy as Face pulled his dick out of her pussy and rammed it into her asshole with force.

"Ahhhhh, shit, nigga I hope you paying for this!" she yelled trying to run from him tearing her asshole into pieces.

After four minutes of anal Face finally, let off a load deep down in her anal and she almost fell on her face as he finally pulled out.

"That was crazy," she said, unable to stand straight.

"Thanks, I got you in the morning with a tip."

"Okay, cool," she said laying in the hotel bed next to him cuddling.

Hours later she woke up and grabbed his pants and wallet on her way to the bathroom. Tatted-up Lust found $4,704 and an AP watch in Face pockets she was gassed up as she placed it all in her purse. She walked back into the room to see him still asleep, she climbed in the bed looking at the clock to see that it was 3:57 a.m. She planned to leave at 6:00 a.m. before he got up so she could have a smooth getaway.

Caught you slipping, nigga, she thought as she went to sleep, and she was a deep sleeper.

***

Two hours later the alarm on her G-shock watch went off, she woke up yawning, then slowly slid out the bed looking for her dress and heels seeing nothing. She thought she was tripping, she crept around the room looking for her shit.

Tatted Up Lust stopped and turned to look at Face about to wake him and to ask him if he'd seen her clothes. When she saw he was gone she went crazy and turned on the room lights.

"No, this nigga didn't!" she yelled as if she was talking to a third person.

She searched the room naked discovering that her purse, phone, keys, money, and clothes were all gone, even her thongs. She wanted to cry, she couldn't believe a nigga had just robbed her. She used the hotel phone to call her friend she worked at the club with to come get her. She hung up and saw a napkin under the lamp with a note on it that read:

Bitch you thought I was sweet. You stinking, pussy ass bitch! LOL!

She cried harder as she wrapped her body in hotel sheets remembering that she didn't get his name, if she had his name, she would send her brothers after him. All her money she made last night was gone. She was dead broke now.

Romell Tukes

Chapter 5

Days Later

Smitty left his house in Harvey, IL outside of Chicago where he lived with his wife and his ten-year-old twin daughters. Smitty was in his BMW X5M with four bricks of Molly in his secret stash spot in the trunk he had put in last month because he was always getting pulled over.

In Chicago getting pulled over for driving while black was a big thing especially if you were in a luxury car. If a nigga didn't have to worry about CPS or jack boys coming for his head, then it was the police.

He was on his way to meet his best client Lil BD. He liked the kid because he was on his grind and about his business. Smitty had his hands in everything; he was a full-time hustler and now with Ty home, he knew they were about to take it to another level. He knew Ty had a major connect who used to bless Ty heavy with so much weight they could flood Chicago. Smitty believed his plug was in Miami because they used to always go out there to re-up.

To be real he didn't care who his plug was as long as Ty was back on because that meant he was on top. He was tired of selling grams and onions and getting work from young Spanish niggas from the Westside of the city.

Smitty re-upped from a nigga name C. Boy who was moving a lot of weight. There were only a couple of people names ringing bells in the city for selling weight King Mike, Boss, C. Boy, and Trey. Smitty knew who King Mike was and C. Boy but he had no clue who Boss or Troy was, and he didn't care because he was willing to do whatever to get back on top. He used to re-up from Face until he disappeared most niggas say the Chi 'Raq Gangstas killed him.

Over the years, he'd been hearing Chi'raq Gangstas a lot about how they viciously murdered Kingpins and well-known gangstas with a bag. He made a mental note to pull Ty's collar about them niggas so they could keep their grass cut low.

The BMW pulled into Denny's restaurant parking to see Lil BD on his phone leaning on his nice ass car with the top down.

In Chi-Town, you had to be an unknown killer and well-respected to ride around with your top-down without getting your head blown off.

"BD, what's good, my guy?" Smitty said as Lil BD came to his window tossing a brown paper bag full of money.

"I'm good, Stone. How are you?" Lil BD said as Smitty tossed the money under his seat trusting Lil BD's math and honor because he always came right.

Smitty went to his trunk and got the four bricks of Molly for him.

"This only four, I know you paid for ten of them thangs. I'ma get right in a couple of hours. So, I'ma hit you," Smitty handed Lil BD a black bag with four keys of Molly rocked up.

"Okay, cool Joe. Just hit me," Lil BD said walking off knowing his plug word was good.

***

Downtown Chicago

Ty was in the gym lifting light weights while doing super setting with weighted pull-ups and dips. The gym was a private gym, so it was normally empty, unlike Planet Fitness or Golds Gym which was full around the clock. He wore a Muscle Gang Fitness tank top and shorts as he got his pump on waiting for Smitty.

Minutes later, Smitty walked in ready to exercise in his work-out Nike Gear with a headband around his big head.

"I know we getting old, but I'm sure headbands been out of style twenty years ago," Ty said lifting 50-pound dumbbells.

Smitty grabbed the 100s. "I don't change with the time," Smitty replied in his deep voice and Ty laughed.

"Good news we back on, I went to holler at my plug and everything is everything. I already got the work in a secure location."

"That's what I'm talking about," Smitty cheered.

"Now we just need to figure out where we're going to move our work because I'ma play the background while you run the show."

"I know, we good. I got clientele already, Ty no worries," Smitty added.

Ty nodded. "A'ight I can't afford no slips because I know the feds still on me. Once you go fed you always fed bound," Ty stated honestly.

"Facts, but I just want to warn you about a crew called Chi Raq Gangstas. They've been out here killing anything or body out here seeing any type of money," Smitty said seriously.

Ty went back to doing pull-ups with a weight belt. "Smitty, how long you known me? You honestly think I'm worried about some little kids?" Ty said.

"They could be old heads for all we know. Niggas say these niggas are like ghost shadows," Smitty said hoping he listened because the streets weren't how it was twenty years ago.

"Them niggas know who to play with, Joe."

"True but this new generation lives by a different code."

"I got a son to handle them little niggas."

"How is Lil Ty Jr?" Smitty said.

"He good. He got a little car lot across town," Ty said.

"Good, he's a good kid. I haven't seen him in years," Smitty said "How's Janelle's sexy ass? I heard she's still a show stopper."

"Smitty, don't push it but I haven't seen her. I'd rather stay focused on this paper." Ty tried to change the subject because Janelle was a soft topic.

He and his baby's mother had a crazy relationship. They met as young kids, but he still had love for her because she was a different type of woman.

They worked out and put their plan together in full motion so they could reclaim the city.

***

Chicago Heights

Boss was in a project building on Wentworth Street which was a goldmine for selling drugs and his little homie Trey had the area on lock.

"Ay, folk, I still got that money from the last load," Trey said bagging up the keys all over the living room table waiting on C. Boy to come by.

"Don't worry about it, just handle your business. That's three-hundred and fifty keys right there. Half for you and the rest for C. Boy," Boss said.

"I got you," Trey said as he heard a knock at the door knowing who it was.

Trey was a GD from Main Street up the block where all the GDs hung out. He'd known Boss for a while because they used to play football against each other for their middle schools. Trey was a short, stocky nigga with an anger problem and his mouth was disrespectful, but his gun game backed it up.

"Damn, nigga, what the fuck folk?" Trey said, letting C. Boy inside the crib, he was dripping in a Louis Vuitton outfit with LV spikes to match.

C. Boy was a pretty boy nigga who was known for letting his gun bark anywhere for his gang. He was a Latin Disciple with a bag, he and Trey had Chicago Heights and the Westside on lock thanks to Boss supplying them with the best work in town for the lowest prices.

"Boss, what's good, big bro?" C. Boy said, embracing Boss checking out his Rolex Everose Daytona in 24k rose gold, automatic with sub-seconds and chronograph big face watch worth 200k.

"Trying to get to this check, bro, but how're the guys?" Boss asked.

"Everybody good, fam. The guys been beefing with the Maniacs and the Mickey Cogwell niggas," C. Boy added as Trey handed him his duffle bag.

"Damn, Joe, it's time to get money fuck the beef shit niggas need to grow up," Boss said and both men agreed.

C. Boy was Trey's friend, he'd put him on with Boss since he was already coping heavyweight from them Detroit niggas before they got knocked by the feds.

"We out," C. Boy said to Trey.

Everybody's phone was going off, they were missing big money.

Romell Tukes

Chapter 6

Downtown, Chi-Town

Janelle hopped out of her Range Rover early in the morning on her way inside her bank to deposit some money. She wore a pair of leggings and a sports bra under her windbreaker jacket. She looked amazing with her flat stomach, thick thighs, phat ass, and beautiful, flawless, butter pecan skin. Her bright, hazel eyes and long clean, neat dreads gave her a youthful look that helped her pass for twenty instead of forty-one years old.

"Good morning," a young man said opening the door for her with two Cuban link necklaces around his neck and he wore a Nike Tech sweatsuit. He was a tall, handsome, well-built dark-skinned brother with long braids.

"Thank you," Janelle said looking at him

"You're beautiful, if I had you, I'll give up everything I ever loved," he said looking at her perfect body and model material face.

"Sweet, but I like men, not boys and money don't make a man."

"I been a man before I started getting money," he replied with a boost in his voice.

"Oh, yeah. So, what's the difference between a boy and a man please don't say it's what's between his legs," she said as civilians walked in and out of the bank as she stood at the open door waiting for his answer

Everywhere she went she got lots of attention from all types of men, she was used to it. Some would get disrespectful, but she would keep it pushing because niggas weren't on her level at all. She'd never met one nigga who was, not even Ty.

"A boy does what he's told, and a man do as he pleases," he said smiling.

"Cute but no the difference if a boy's brain isn't mentally mature to understand the reality of life and his growth will come with life lessons. Now a man is the maker of his own success and destruction. He knows the difference between his own values and morals. He molds himself into a king once he realizes the crown was always on his head. A boy will never see this because he can't think past *go*. All he sees is cars, jewelry, clothes, fast women, and overnight success and fame," she said.

The young man didn't know what to say knowing she was far out of his league. "Thank you," he said honestly.

"Sure, just don't short your life by focusing on meaningless things and people," she educated.

He nodded. She had no clue the young man she was talking to sold drugs for her son, Boss. The young man walked off having a newfound respect for the woman whose name he didn't even know. He just knew that her beauty and intelligence were on another level.

Janelle waited in line thinking about her conversation with the young man. She saw so much loss in his brown eyes, she felt it was needed to break down the true meaning of the creation of men. She still worked at the school as a History teacher and she'd got a second job at a detention center to speak to the youth. She kept herself busy and with Boss and Lil BD living their lives she had nothing but free time.

At least six to eight times a year she would go on trips or cruises to places like Cabo Verde, Barbados, the Caribbean, and her birthplace Haiti with her girls. Her love life sucked but she was cool with her toy, she knew her toy couldn't give her no type of disease or talk back. She'd heard from Boss that his father was home. She was happy for Ty, but he'd been history to her emotionally. Before Ty went to prison, he was running the streets having his bitches call their home and he would sometimes abuse her. She was at a weak point in her life back then, she was young, dumb, and full of pain.

When he got locked up, they agreed to be cool and focus on Boss. Since he'd been locked up, she never once denied him a relationship with Boss as most females would have done after all the fucked-up shit, he did to her.

Janelle put 6500 in her bank and made her way to the track to get her morning jog and exercise in as she did five days a week to stay fit and healthy.

***

Cook County Jail

Boss was in the large, packed jail visiting area for Malik's 22nd birthday. Plus, Malik said he needed to speak to him. Boss looked around to see all the young niggas locked up and he felt their pain and grief because he was once in their shoes but he refused to wear the same shoes twice.

After thirty minutes of waiting Malik finally came out with muscles busting out of his prison uniform. What Boss realized that shocked him the most was that Malik had cut off his dreads.

"Bro, what's good?" Malik hugged Boss as they embraced tightly before sitting down.

"You got your fucking weight up, Joe. What you be doing in here all day, pushups, nigga?" Boss said laughing.

"Somewhat, a nigga gotta stay war-ready."

"I see. Why you cut the dreads, Lord?" Boss asked, looking at his waves spinning.

"I just felt like it was time for a change, bro. I've been so focused on the trial I had no time to work on me mentally because I'd been physically drained."

"I feel you, bro, but niggas still miss you."

"You the bro, I don't give a fuck about anybody else. To be honest, niggas ain't solid to me," Malik said referring to his Vice Lord homies.

"I hear you."

"Good looking on that situation. I almost lost my life in this bitch. I died twice, a nigga thought I saw Allah," Malik said laughing.

"No problem. Shit, any nigga that puts money on your head. Puts money on my head as well. But the way he begged for his life made me and Animal laugh in tears." Boss said laughing thinking back to when he killed S. Lord for getting Malik stabbed up in the jail.

"How is he?" Malik said looking at a couple of inmates watching him.

"Animal good, bro, he be outta town checking a bag but he in the hood now chilling with his guys."

"A'ight, that's what's popping. How's the car lot?"

"Shit looking good and Rosie's hair salon is the hottest hair shop in the city, bro, she lit."

"That's good, bro, I'm proud of you. How's your pops doing?"

"This nigga got a new Mercedes, a new condo, all designer shit. This nigga came home touching a bag," Boss said.

"All the old heads be talking about him like he's God in this bitch."

"Yeah, speaking of the most-high. I've been going to Jumah and fucking with Iman Sa`id. I think I'ma take my shahada soon," Boss said seriously.

Becoming a Muslim had been on his mind for years the only thing stopping him was him being heavy in the streets living a life of sin.

"My boy about to be Muslim, okay, ahkee. I can't front, bro, the whole jail on their deen, I was born Muslim."

"We all were born Muslim but we grow into other religions. The white men religion our ancestors were forced into during the time of slavery."

"You sound like your mom mixed with a little Malcolm X," Malik said laughing but knowing Boss was telling the truth.

"Whatever, but you know my mom be talking that shit."

"She's a Black Panther, nigga. How is she and BD?"

"She's good, looking younger than us both. BD, bro, I can't speak on, because I don't know, but I hear he's doing good in Buff City."

"I start trial in a couple of months. This DA nigga he's not even trying to give me a cop-out, bro. He's trying to put my lights out by killing both of these cops. They don't have no type of strong evidence on me," Malik said.

"What your lawyer say?"

"This nigga under pressure, he's worried about the witness statements holding weight at trial."

"What's your DA's name?"

"Mr. Aleksondrov some weird looking Russian, nigga," Malik added.

"A'ight, look, bro, just sit back, chill and be patient, everything's going to fall into place," Boss said as finished their visit.

***

Southside, Chi-Town

Today was Jumah Friday service for Muslims and the Mosque was packed with close to 150 Muslims, males, and females. Everybody was dressed in garments and hijabs and the strong smell of Muslim oil filled the massive size Mosque.

Iman Sa`id was giving the Khutbah a religious ceremony as always.

"Sami Allahu Liman hamidah," Iman Sa`id said in Arabic which meant Allah hears him who praises him in English.

"Today someone is taking his Shahada, his testimony of faith. I've known this man since he was a baby. I pray Allah will guide him. Come up here, Ty," Iman Sa`id said on the mic as Boss stood up from the front row in his white garment.

"Are you sure you're ready to submit your soul to Allah and take an oath to your creator?" Iman asked.

"Yes."

"Good, repeat after me La` ilaha illallah, Muhammad-ur-Rasul-Allah," Iman Sa`id stated as Boss repeated them same words. "Now let's say it in English. None has the right to be worshipped but Allah, and Muhammad is the Messenger of Allah," Iman' Sa`id stated, Boss, repeated the same words. As-salaam-alaikum you're a Muslim now," Iman yelled.

All the brothers embraced Boss as a new Muslim. They were very happy for him.

Romell Tukes

Chapter 7

Mr. Aleksondrov was the head DA in the Cook County and Will County area and has been for the past five years. He was a strong figure in the Chicago court system. His word was golden, he had the power to make cases disappear and reappear. Today was a hot nice day outside so he was out golfing like he's been doing for twenty-years out of his fifty-two years on earth.

He was rich with a beautiful Russian wife from Kaliningrad. Arkadiy who he had a two-year-old daughter with. He lived in Olympia Field, IL in a 19.5 million-dollar, 18,712 square foot mansion with six acres.

"You almost made it," another golfer said who was a Judge. The same judge is trying Malik's case. The two have had a good relationship for over twenty years since they've been golfing buddies.

"Almost is never close. You ready for this trial with the kid who killed them two cops?" Mr. Aleksondrov asked, taking off his Cartier sunglasses showing his glasses tan line.

"I'm just waiting on you," Judge Olson said, who was a racist old man from Alabama and part of the KKK.

"We don't have enough evidence, but I will make it enough."

"Good, we need to get all these niggas off our streets to make America great again," Judge Olsen said seriously sounding like President Trump.

"Indeed, I'll have everything ready in a couple of weeks but I have to go," he said checking his Mint Rolex Day-Date, 40 watch in 18k yellow gold, with a President bracelet and automatic with sweep seconds, date, and day.

"Okay, give me a ring, I'm waiting on my mistress here while my wife is at some spa with her daughter," Judge Olsen said with an evil grin.

"Have fun," Mr. Aleksondrov said walking off in his Polo shorts, collar shirt, and his Polo golfing shoes looking more like a tennis player than a golfer.

In the country club parking lot, he saw a young, black, man leaning his ass on his brand new gray Aston Martin V12 Vintage worth a quarter-million dollars.

"Excuse me, you thug, but you have your fucking ass on my car!" Mr. Aleksondrov shouted.

Boss just looked at him with a folder in his hand. "Oh, I'm sorry," Boss pulled out a .40 caliber handgun.

Aleksondrov jumped back thinking he was about to die.

Boss took the butt of his gun and smashed out the taillights of his Aston Martin. Aleksondrov wanted to cry but he sucked up. This was why he hated black people and did everything in his power to send them all to jail.

"Now listen, you know Malik Fields. I'm sure you do, so there's no need to answer but you will dismiss both of his murder cases at trial," Boss said.

"Have you lost your damn mind? That's not going to happen, his trial is in months."

"Okay, take a look at these pictures and see if you'll change your mind. I'm sure you will," Boss handed him the folder.

Mr. Aleksondrov had an angry, sour look on his face when he saw pictures of his wife and daughter leaving their mansion. He also saw pictures of his mother's nursing home in Riverdale, IL. He knew whoever the kid was he meant business and now seeing his family's lives were at stake he changed his whole attitude.

"Just give me some time, I can't make any promises, he's already in too deep."

"If you think he's in deep." Boss chuckled. "Wait until you see how deep I bury your daughter, alive, while you watch. You got a couple of weeks and don't bother going to the police or running because I also know where to find your niece, two nephews, and your mistress." Boss walked off.

Mr. Aleksondrov had kept his mistress a secret for years. He wondered how Boss knew about her. His mistress was a transgender woman he was deeply in love with, she was black and he was paying big money for all of her surgeries.

He slammed the folder on the hood of his cars, sick and thinking of something because he loved his family but dismissing a case so big would look bad on his resume.

***

Months Later

Ty stone sat in his condo waiting for Smitty to come upstairs; he'd just texted him telling him he was downstairs. Ty and Smitty had the city of Chicago on lock. He was seeing so much money, he had to build safes in his condo. Smitty was the face of the operation as they planned while he supplied the work and collected the money. Within months Ty was back to a millionaire and all he did was sit at home and go to the gym. He took a couple of trips to Vegas and Miami enjoying the finer things of life. He sent Pistol and his man OG Chuck some flicks of him on boats surrounded by women, parties he attended, and he sent them both 100,000 apiece.

Ty could never forget about the niggas who was with him in the struggle that was part of being a real nigga and standing for something. He went to unlock the door for Smitty figuring he was close.

Ty attended his brother's funeral. He'd even paid for the service and carried the casket but it was a very small ceremony of twenty people. What was shocking was when everybody saw a cute, thick, red-headed white chick spit on Jay's fucked up discomposed face.

"Ty," Smitty said with his deep voice.

"What's up? You look upset," Ty said at his minibar pouring himself a cup of Patron

"Make me one too, we got an issue," Smitty said sitting down in the living room out of breath from the flight of stairs he'd just taken.

"Damn, already?"

"My main worker got robbed and Pistol whipped in K-Town on the Westside," Smitty said pissed off his little cousin was in a coma in the hospital.

"How much they take?" Ty asked

"Twenty-seven bricks."

"He had that much shit on him, Joe? Was he trying to get robbed?"

"Nah he was making a run" Smitty defended his cousin.

"We run that hood."

"A GD kid named Trey and his crew be moving a lot of weight over there," Smitty added

"So, he robbed, and pistol-whipped him to send us a message?" Ty said walking into the living room thinking.

"Yeah, we gotta do something, Ty. Or these little niggas gonna roll all over us and start trying to rob us."

"You know this Trey dude?"

"No, but I can find out."

"Good, get back to me. I got a plan but beware our actions can lead to a war with God knows who because this kid could be connected to anybody," Ty said being a thinker.

"Fuck him and who he knows, we war-ready," Smitty said standing up to leave wearing his emotions on his sleeve.

Chapter 8

Jenny and Lil BD were in the living room, eating Chinese takeout and watching Love N Hip-Hop on VH1, laughing at the dirty drama on the TV show.

"You know who I ran into today? That big nigga who used to stay on the same block as you," Lil BD said.

"Oh, the homie Animal?" she replied.

He rubbed his hand on her smooth legs on his lap. "Yeah, he had a nice Bentley. It looks like he was doing it big," Lil BD said.

He used to see Animal here and there, but he didn't know the nigga at all, except that he was a BD under Loso just like he was.

"I heard he was out of town chasing a bag. Me and him got a lot of history," she said as if it was nothing.

Lil BD stared at her. "You what?" he said so she could repeat it.

"Not like that, Justin. Me and him did a lot of business. I never slept with him, you know I don't get down like that," she said.

"What business did you have with him then?"

"When he came home, he was asking questions about the nigga Loso. I had a friend who was fucking with Loso, so she gave me some information. I sold it to him, period. I didn't fuck with Loso, he was a snake and he was all for self. I saw that nigga rat on Tombs that night he killed Loso's little brother," she said.

He couldn't believe what he just heard. "How come you never said nothing?"

"Everybody was on his dick because he was blinded by the money."

"That was my big homie, I looked up to him. To hear he was a rat and you helped set him up, just makes me look at you different."

"What?" she yelled

"I ain't know you was out here crossing niggas."

"First off, I ain't cross nobody. I could've given two fucks about that rat ass nigga. I ain't kill him the Chi Raq Gangstas did. Don't be mad at me," she said with an attitude.

"Animal down with them niggas?" Lil BD said surprised that a BD was down with the deadliest crew in the city. "I thought it was all Vice Lords since the kid Malik got caught for the cop killings," Lil BD said confused.

"No, it's only three of them, Animal, Malik, and a dude named Boss," she said, still mad he was trying to make her out to be a grimy bitch.

"Boss?"

"Yeah, some GD nigga I believe. I think he runs the crew, at least that's what Animal said one night when he was drunk," Jenny said, seeing a crazy look on his face. "You okay, babe?"

"Boss?"

"Yeah. Why, do you know him? Baby, please leave them niggas alone they're dangerous," she said as she continued to talk as if he didn't hear a word come out her mouth.

It all started to make sense to him now. How Boss made it to the top so fast he was part of the Chi Raq Gangstas. Lil BD always wondered who was behind the crew's vicious murders all around Chicago.

"That's my brother," he admitted.

She looked more shocked than him. She even forgot he had a brother because he never talked about him.

"You sure?" she said wishing she would've kept her mouth closed but she was honest with him.

"I gotta go, I'll be back later." He leaned in and kissed her as he got up in a rush.

Jenny prayed he didn't wake up a laying dog because she knew the Chi'Raq Gangstas was on another level with drilling shit, the whole city did.

***

Downtown, Chi-Town

"Kylie, how did we do today on car sales?" Boss asked his assistant and best saleswomen at his car lot.

"We did good, the new salesman got rid of six cars today and me twelve," she said smiling showing her new, white teeth.

"Good job," Boss turned and exited his office in his Gucci slacks and Valentino button-up looking professional as he did every time he came to his place of business.

Kylie followed him to his luxury office upstairs. "Boss, I just want to say thank you," Kylie said with her head down as her long red hair hung down her lower back.

"For what?"

"For everything. You helped me get my life back. I went from smoking crack, selling pussy for Jay's bitch ass, to rehab. Now I've bought a house and I'm driving a new Benz coupe," she said smiling.

Kylie a.k.a Red Head went to rehab for almost a year when Boss told her she was lost in the streets and hopelessly chasing dope and crack.

"You should be proud of yourself, you came a long way. Now get back to work, I got a client coming. Just send him up here," Boss said.

She showed him her beautiful smile before she walked off and her Fendi outfit hugged her curves making her look like a snack.

Twenty minutes later, King Mike walked into Boss' office and three of his soldiers waited downstairs outside picking out two new cars because they had a crazy shootout last night in their two SUVs parked outside.

"This shit is nice, Boss. You're doing your thing," King Mike said sitting down in a gold and black Versace outfit looking like a smooth pretty boy pimp.

"Thanks, this shit doing good."

"Good to hear, but I brought them two Yukon trucks for you outside. Everything is in the back of each truck four-hundred keys in each," King Mike said.

"A'ight, I'ma have my people drop the money off at your requested location."

"No rush but I do need two new cars. We had a little shoot last night with some old nigga in L-Town trying to demand my block," King Mike said with a laugh.

Boss shook his head glad he didn't have to deal with no street beef.

"Pick whatever whips you want on the house."

"Nah, man, I support the hustler."

"You supported enough, bro, grab whatever cars you want."

"Okay, I'ma get going. Send my sister my love, and my wife went to her salon with her niece, but she wasn't there yesterday."

"We were in New York celebrating our anniversary," Boss said as King Mike nodded and left.

***

Westside, Chi-Town

Trey was creeping out of one of the trap building making sure his little homies wasn't fucking up his money. It was past midnight and the streets were dark and empty. Trey had plans to slide over to Melissa's crib who lived in Holy City because she was blowing his phone up, talking about she was ready to fuck. When she sent her Cash App number with a request for $1000 he knew she had him fucked up as if he was a trick. Trey had an orange Maserati GranTurismo Coupe SP with tints he had the brightest car in the hood, but everybody admired it.

Last week Trey had to pistol-whip a nigga for trying to sell drugs in his neighborhood he didn't play no games when it came to his turf. L-Town and K-Town was a money-making gold mine and it was all his and the Kings' turf.

Bloc! Bloc! Bloc! Bloc! Bloc! Bloc!

Trey was hit in his lower back in the middle of the street as he used the strength of his upper body to crawl to the Maserati where his Draco was.

"Don't run little nigga," a deep voice said now standing over Trey as he gritted in pain.

Smitty kicked him in his stomach and Ty walked up with his gun in hand with a mask on.

"Who you work for?" Ty asked.

"Your mother," Trey spat with a smirk.

Bloc! Bloc! Bloc! Bloc!

Ty shot him four times in the upper torso as he and Smitty walked off and climbed in a Tahoe truck.

By the time Trey's goons came out, he was dead on the street and sirens were nearby. Trey's aunty screams could be heard from blocks away as she ran outside and saw him poured out on the ground.

Romell Tukes

Chapter 9

Olympia Field, IL

"Uggghhh yesssss!" Arkadly cried out as she straddled low onto her husband's nice size dick.

She began slowly riding his dick so Mr. Aleksondrov grabbed her thin, petite waist as her little butt bounced on his thighs. Arkadly was a Russian bombshell, tall, skinny with blue eyes, blonde hair, and nice, B cup breasts. She was born and raised in Russia where she was a model until she met Aleksondrov who was twenty-seven years older than her. He gave her the world and she fell for his money, so she got married and had a beautiful daughter two years ago.

"Fuck me harder! Make me cum!" she yelled in her Russian accent, placing her hands on his chest and bouncing up and down swinging her hair.

Mr. Aleksondrov felt himself about to cum as his dick worked in and out of her wet gushy pussy that had the tightest grip ever.

She placed a finger in her asshole as he wrapped both arms around her frail waist and started to pound her pussy up.

"Yesssss!" she yelled as he rammed his dick deep into her little pussy, she caught a crazy orgasm on his dick. "Uhmmmm," she moaned as he sucked on her little pink nipple.

"I'm about to—" he came inside his wife as she grinded on his cock while he filled her up with thick cum until he went limp inside her.

Arkadly wanted more so she kissed his lip and neck trying to heat him up again. She was on her way down south to deepthroat every inch. She had no gag reflex so her head game was top of the line, it drove niggas crazy to the point that she had many stalkers.

Aleksondrov closed his eyes, meditating and enjoying the show, his wife's oral sex was the reason he'd married her.

Whack!

The pistol slapped Arkadiy so hard her body flew off the bed to the other side of the room. Aleksondrov jumped up naked and scared to death until Boss crashed his pistol over his head.

"Sit your bitch ass down," Boss said dressed in all black while Animal held Arkadly at gunpoint.

Boss had been waiting for Malik's cases to be dismissed but every time he asked Malik what was going on with his cases over the phone, he had no updates. Boss didn't tell Malik what he was up to, just in case shit went left but he was sure his plan would work.

"I'm sorry please don't kill my wife or me. I've been trying to get the cases dropped but I need more time," Mr. Aleksondrov pleaded, looking at his wife in the fetal position crying for her life, with a swollen face, wondering what he'd gotten her into.

"Your time is up cracker." Boss cocked his Desert Eagle and shoving it in the DA's mouth.

His eyes almost popped out his head.

"Please don't—" Arkadly cried.

Animal punched her in her swollen face and she went to sleep while blood spilled out her mouth. Boss only hoped Animal hadn't killed the skinny, cute snow bunny.

"This is what I'ma do because I'ma good guy. When Malik's trial date appears you will fuck the case up, lie, convince the jury and judge it wasn't him," Boss said looking into the man's fearful eyes as he nodded his head since he couldn't talk because the gun was still in her throat. "Good now suck on the gun, nigga," Boss said. Aleksondrov sucked the barrel of the gun. "Suck harder!" Boss yelled, Aleksondrov sucked harder up and down with tears.

Boss and Animal couldn't help but laugh as his wife woke up trying to move until Animal knocked her out again.

"Come on, bro, you gonna kill the bitch."

"Maybe," Animal shrugged..

"Just so we have a clear understanding, I'll be taking your wife and daughter to a secured location until Malik is released. Then you'll get your family back," Boss said.

Animal picked up his wife's naked body and tossed her over his broad shoulders.

"Please, you don't have to do that! I will have the cases dismissed," he begged.

"I know you will but until you do—" Boss walked out of his room, headed into his daughter's room to take her while she was sound asleep.

Mr. Aleksondrov was in the bed crying a river, regretting taking the big case, thinking it would brighten his career. In reality, he had no hardcore evidence to convict Malik, he just knew the right people in the right places. When he heard his sliding back door close in his kitchen he looked out of his window to see his wife and kid being taken away in an all-black GMC truck with tints.

***

Robins, IL

Ty pulled into the driveway of a small, yellow house directly on the highway on eight acres of land. To most people, this would be considered the country but Ty used to come here to get peace of mind and get his thoughts together. He'd brought this property years before he was sent off to prison, luckily, he was smart enough to put it in Janelle's name around the time they got serious. Ty made his way to the back of the house toward the rundown, metal shed. The grass was extremely high making the backyard look like a cornfield.

Inside the shed, he moved some tools, a chair, and an old dusty rug covering a secret latch that led into the private basement area he had installed years ago. Ty lifted the flood panel and used the ladder that led into the dark basement tunnel. He turned on the rusty light which still works to see bricks stacked up six-feet high covering a whole wall.

This was Ty's life savings nobody knew about, not even Smitty because in the dope game the one closest to you would cross you for the love of the money, a green piece of paper. This was Ty's second trip back to his stash since he'd been home, while he told Smitty he was going to see his plug which was a lie because he was the plug. Ty didn't have a plug in years, his last plug couldn't be trusted and the plug before that tried to kill him.

Ty had to load up his car with 270 keys then he would have Smitty meet him in a public place where they could switch cars. Riding around with 270 bricks wasn't smart but he had no choice if he wanted to remain a step ahead of the game.

**

Buff City

Animal was coming out of his mom's house with his annoying sister, who needed a ride to the store. He tried to move his mom out of the hood, but she refused to leave. He and his mom had a rough, crazy relationship as well as his sister Whitney.

"Let me get some money," Whitney walked toward his Bentley. She wore a Juicy sweatsuit with her hair wrapped in a scarf. She was tall and dark-skinned, with an overbite, thick and loud. Every nigga who was getting money had fucked her once before until she started burning niggas. Now at thirty-years-old, she was working at Western Union still living with her mom who sniffed coke all day and got drunk.

"I just gave you a band," Animal stated, seeing how dark it was so early outside as he walked around his Bentley.

"I went shopping, nigga. You getting all this money but can't trick on your sister?"

"Nigga, that's because I'm not a trick. You better find a sugar daddy like all these other thots!"

"Boy, whatever, open the door," she said standing at the passenger door.

They saw an all-black Callaway Tahoe bulletproof truck creep down the street with the HD lights.

Boc! Boc! Boc! Boc! Boc! Boc! Boc! Boc! Boc!

Animal pulled out his .357 and shot back while ducking as bullets put holes in his Bentley. Animal saw the gunman's face and couldn't believe who it was. He let off two more shots hitting the truck but leaving no damages. The truck sped off bending the corner.

"Come on, Whitney," Animal said looking for his sister who he thought was still ducking because shootouts in the hood were regular shit.

When he heard no reply, he walked around the car to see his sister laid out on the curb in a puddle of blood with two holes in her head the size of nickels.

"Damn it—fuckkk!" he yelled.

His mom ran outside to see what the fuck was going on. When she saw her daughter laid out dead on the curb she felt as if she was in a nightmare wishing it was Animal dead instead.

"Nooooo—not, my baby!" his mom cried, then she kneeled down crying over her daughter's dead body.

Animal knew he couldn't stick around so he hopped in his Bentley and pulled off before Chicago PD arrived. Animal couldn't get the image of Face out of his head. He'd tried to take his life just now but he promised he would pay for his sister's death.

Romell Tukes

Chapter 10

Cook County Jail

Malik was in his cell reading *Murda Season 2* by *Lock Down Publications* author *Romell Tukes* feeling as if he was in a movie. He didn't normally read books until late night but he couldn't put this book down. His trial was coming up in a couple of weeks and to say he was ready was an understatement. He couldn't sleep or focus because his life was in the white man's hands who hated Black America. He spoke to Boss every day it was good to have him in his corner but lately, he was always asking about the status of his case, and Malik hated talking about the trial when he called the outside world.

Every day he missed his mom and stepdad who was killed on his behalf by B. Stone. He never told Simone about the Face situation because he didn't want to make her feel as if she had to pick between him or her family. Malik saw his man Lil D at his door waving for him to come over. Malik put on his prison sneakers and walked out of his cell to hear rare silence. Whenever a dorm was silent something was about to go down any second.

"What up, Lil D?"

"Your celly upstairs in the TV room on bullshit at the dice game," Lil D said.

Malik took a deep breath and made his way upstairs where inmates would shoot dice, fight, smoke, and exercise. When Malik walked into the room, he saw Ra Ra stripping three dudes, ass naked with a big knife in his hand. The three dudes on the wall looked like they were about to cry.

"Ra, what the fuck you doing?" Malik said, snapping Ra Ra out of his trance, seeing fire in his young eyes.

"These goofy ass niggas tried to trick the dice by using these," Ra Ra said tossing Malik the fake dice.

Other inmates surrounded the room some were laughing and some were scared for their homies because they all knew Ra Ra was a vicious nigga.

Malik saw the dice and Ra Ra was right the dice were fake made for winning. "What you gonna do, bro? Because if you hit these niggas up, they gonna shake the block down and lock you up again," Malik said talking some sense into his celly because he was the only one who could.

"All three of y'all check-in if y'all come back to this block I'ma kill y'all niggas," Ra Ra said.

All the men ran out of the room naked running to the C.O. 's booth telling him they were checking in which meant going to a P.C. unit, Protected Custody.

Ra Ra collected all the food stamps, and clothes on the floor, Malik helped, and ten inmates watched.

"Y'all niggas got a problem?" Ra Ra said looking at the inmates who wanted to stick up for their homies he'd just violated but they knew better.

"Nah, we good you need some help," a BD kid asked before everybody went downstairs gossiping about what had happened.

***

Westside, Chi-Town

It was a chilly day outside, Smitty sat in his truck watching his new block do numbers, smiling like a kid on Christmas morning. Smitty took over Trey's block after he and Ty killed him. The next day he came back to the block with six goons giving niggas packs and telling them to report to him and his guys every Friday.

One nigga tried to protest until Smitty's goons pulled out Dracos, then he got with the program.

Smitty was running through at least 50 keys a day, the fiends say it's the best crack they've had in years of smoking. Smitty knew all fiends would say anything just to get a free tester but whoever Ty's plug was he prayed he continued to bless him.

He saw two fiends on the corner in a vicious fistfight blow for blow, even when the police arrived, they were still getting it in. Soldiers were on every corner and every section of the block selling his shit. He knew it wouldn't be long before he and Ty had the city on lock but first he needed an army.

Smitty had a couple of little cousins and nephews on his squad but he needed to recruit some killers just in case the Chi Raq Gangstas surfaced again, that was his only worry.

***

Downtown, Chi-Town

Boss was at work walking around in his car lot checking out the new Lexus and Range Rover that had arrived making sure everything was intact and no parts were missing. A lot of times when he would get new cars there would be a dent somewhere or a missing windshield wiper, even missing or damaged bumpers. Boss had been putting a lot of time into his car lot which was doing great. He had over 300 cars in the lot and twenty brand new luxury cars not even out yet in the USA on the showroom floor.

Trap money kinda slowed down since Trey was murdered last month but C. Boy was holding shit down and not to mention he had a couple of big spenders out in VA and D.C. who came up once a month to re-up.

Boss saw a red Ferrari 488 GTB Coupe enter the parking lot slowly. C. Boy hopped out in a Burberry outfit with Burberry boots to match. There was a beautiful Asian chick in the passenger seat fixing her lipstick.

"C. Boy, I see you stepping your game up?"

"I'm just a snail in the game, bro, but check game. We got a little issue. Some niggas took over Trey's block and turned that shit into the Wire," C. Boy said as Boss listened.

"You know who they are?"

"Nah, not yet. Trey's little homie pulled up to my block yesterday talking about how some older, big, gorilla-looking nigga hopped out on his guys giving them packs to sale."

"They took it," Boss said surprisingly

"Yeah, youngin' said them niggas had poles ready to drill some shit."

"Damn, this shit don't make sense, these must be some outta town niggas. Because niggas respect the land and turfs. Now they violating GD because that's my turf. Look, find out whatever you can about these niggas and report to me. These niggas maybe responsible for Trey's death," Boss said.

"Got you, me, and my guys with you. Oh, yeah, and Trey's little homie told me they was told to report every Friday to drop off their weekly gross and re-up."

"Good, perfect," Boss said, already coming up with an idea.

First, he had to meet with Animal because he'd been sick since the death of his sister. Boss hadn't made time to see Animal yet but he told Boss he needed to speak to him as fast as possible. Tonight, after work he planned to meet Animal at Lincoln Park same as they used to do daily before they went on missions as the Chi 'Raq Gangstas. Boss had the DA's wife and daughter in a rented boat parked on a boat dock on a waterfront in Chatham.

Chapter 11

Oak Park, IL

The gray Cadillac CTS-V was parked on the corner of the quiet middle-class neighborhood outside of Chicago as darkness filled the sky.

"Did you feed the bitch and baby?" Boss asked Animal as they watched the brick house with the manicured cut grass and a three-car garage.

"Nigga, miss me with that," Animal replied with an attitude. "You know I fed that bitch."

Boss knew he was still upset because he had to bury his sister this morning, so he paid his attitude no mind but before his sister passed he'd been acting unusual.

When Animal told Boss about Face popping up again, he knew if they didn't get rid of him fast he would become a big irritation. Boss went to go see Malik and told him about Face. So, he had Malik ask Simone about his baby mothers and she talked so much she gave him the addresses to where all of them lived.

Malik called Boss with the good news, now he was on a mission to find Face while waiting on Malik's trial date. Boss still kept it a secret about making a deal with the DA because he wanted to surprise his boy.

"This goofy nigga ain't coming. You ready?" Animal asked while closely scrutinizing the house where one of Face's baby mother's lived with their four kids.

"Whenever you're ready, big boy," Boss said as Animal pulled his mask down and grabbed a 9mm Glock with a thirty round clip attached to it.

"Follow me," Animal instructed.

Boss hopped out of the car creeping across the street into the back of the house where they saw a red nose pitbull sleeping.

"Shhhh," Boss whispered as Animal black Timbs stomped on tree branches making noise. There was an entrance for the dog to come and go as he pleased inside the house.

Boss and Animal looked at each other because the dog door was the only way to get inside, so one of them had to squeeze in the small slot. Boss was a lot smaller so he went for it, cutting his arms and thigh but after ten minutes of struggling, he was in the kitchen.

When he unlocked the door, Animal saw a piece of Boss' dreadlock on the floor causing him to laugh. Boss went crazy over his dreads. Boss picked up the long dreadlock that got ripped off as he tried to climb inside the dog entrance.

"Ain't nothing to sew back on," Boss said, shoving it in his pocket.

Boss and Animal walked into the living room to see a dark-skinned, thick woman, with short hair laying on the couch sleep in a blanket.

Bloc! Bloc! Bloc! Bloc! Bloc!

Animal killed her with five shots to the face. Boss just looked at her lifeless body as her head hung off the armrest.

Boss heard a door open upstairs, he saw Animal rush up the staircase and he followed with his gun drawn. At the top of the stairs, they were face to face with four black, ass ugly kids who looked African. Without hesitation, Animal shot all four of the kids in the head with no type of remorse.

"I feel a little better. Come on let's get out of here. You ain't even have to put no work in tonight," Animal said joking as he walked downstairs.

The pit bull ran toward them about to attack Boss.

Boc! Boc!

Boss shot the dog in his head as the dog's body rolled down the stairs.

"Just did," Boss said exiting the front door shaking their heads.

***

Cook County Court

Today was Malik's trial date, he was sitting in the courtroom packed with people and news reporters. He saw Boss sitting in the back smiling, he wished he could smile too but he couldn't bring himself to it.

Malik wore an all-black Armani suit and tie with a pair of Stacy Adams shoes and a pair of Cartier glasses. He had a C.O. sneak in the jail for him last week.

"Something strange is going on but just roll with the punches," his lawyer said, sitting back smoking a vapor as the courts got started with open arguments.

Malik's lawyer went first explaining to the jury how his client was innocent.

"As you see the DA has no witnesses or footage of Mr. Fields committing any of these gruesome murders. America is the land of freedom, equality, and justice, am I correct? I'm sure my client has done nothing wrong, whatsoever. My client was being investigated for a chain of robberies by Detective Rodriguez before his body was found. How in the world can my client be charged for his murder? He had no clue he was even being investigated. I'm sure there are thousands of convictions Detective Rodriguez has made that could have gotten him an enemy. The detective had over thirty harassment complaints, let's be fair here, this is a young black man in white America from the worst section of Chicago.

These young black men are never given a fair chance but let's be fair today and justice needs to be set, thank you," Malik's lawyer stated as a couple of blacks in the crowd clapped.

"Mr. Aleksondrov, your turn," Judge Olsen said as the DA stood up to present his case, unable to look at Malik.

"From everything I could come up with we don't have no solid proof to convict Mr. Fields of any murder of any type. We went off a statement that became a conflict of interest, so we can't use that in the court of law. I'm sorry but Mr. Fields is as innocent as they come," Mr. Aleksondrov said before sitting down and the court went up in chaos.

Judge Olsen couldn't believe what he'd just heard, he had no choice but to dismiss this case.

"Wow, I have no choice but to dismiss this case, but Mr. Fields is to be held in the county jail for a suspended license ticket." Judge

Olsen banged his gavel, then he called Mr. Aleksondrov to the back to speak to him. He needed to see what the fuck had just happened. Not only had Aleksandrov made the courtroom look bad but he made himself look like a fool.

Boss saw Malik look at him with a smile knowing his boy had something to do with what had just happened. The court police led Malik to the back bullpens to send him back to jail to do time for a ticket which was only for a couple of days since he had time in already.

Chapter 12

Chatham, Chi-Town

Boss and Animal were in the boat waiting on Aleksandrov to show up to get his family since he'd done his part and got Malik's case dismissed.

"Is my husband coming to get us?" Arkadly stated, she was chained and cuffed to a bed rail while her daughter was sleeping in a baby carriage next to her.

"I hope so because you and your daughter smell like shit," Boss said walking out of the room, closing the door behind. He saw Aleksondrov's Aston Martin pull up outside and Animal was waiting to pat him down and see if he was being followed.

Arkadly and her daughter couldn't use the restroom, they had to piss and shit on themselves, but Boss made sure he never cuffed Arkadly's left hand so she could cater to her child. He also left a box of wipes next to her head for whenever needed.

Boss saw Animal escorting Aleksandrov onto the boat dock with a nervous look on his face.

"Nice to see you made it," Boss said smiling.

Aleksondrov stepped inside the boat smelling the strong odor that took his breath away.

"I did my part, your friend is free of all charges. Can I have my family back?"

"Sure, but are you sure you didn't tell a soul? Because I would hate to come back for you and your family," Boss threatened seriously.

"I swear I didn't tell a soul. I would never put my family in that type of position. I just want this to be over," Aleksondrov said.

"It's over tonight you did a good job. Come get your famil.," Boss patted him on his back, leading him into the back room where the strong odor of shit and urine was coming from.

When Aleksondrov entered the room, he saw his wife on the floor chained and cuffed to the bed.

"Oh, my Goddd, baby!" Akradly cried out happy to see him for the first time in her young life.

"You're okay," he said, feeling her strong face and high cheekbones. He saw his daughter peacefully sleeping.

"I missed you so much," she cried.

"It's okay we're leaving, right now," he said as he stood up stepping his $3700 shoes in urine. "You can uncuff her and we'll be out of your way," Aleksondrov said to Boss who was standing at the doorway watching them reunite which made him smile knowing how important family is.

"I'm sorry, Mr. Aleksondrov, but I can't do that. You know too much about me and my guys," Boss said calmly.

Animal stood ten feet behind him wishing he would just hurry the fuck up and kill them.

"What! You promised me, my family, back!" he shouted turning beet red.

"No, I ain't promise you shit. This is how it goes, now you know how it feels when you convict a lot of my people and give them life in prison."

"I never gave anybody anything unless I felt they deserved it. This is why I hate all of you niggers!" Aleksondrov shouted out of anger.

"There goes your true, divine creed." Boss pulled out his gun, shooting him in the head.

His wife screamed as his body collapsed on top of hers, he shot her six times in her breasts. The baby's cries were so loud, Boss had no choice but to fire a round in the baby's chest.

"You ain't leave none for me," Animal said seriously seeing everybody in the room dead.

"You need help, bro. You taking this killing shit to the head. It's only a job, it's like you're falling in love with this shit," Boss said as they left the boat.

Animal didn't say a word because Boss was correct at night, he would dream about killing people. Sometimes he would cum after killing someone but he was starting to think it was normal.

***

Washington Park

It was a nice, windy Sunday in the park as Boss and Ty played their sixth basketball game one on one full court. Boss was shocked to see that his pops had a six-pack, defined arms, and chest with his shirt off.

"Come on, young boy. You tired already?" Ty said, passing his son the basketball, he played defense as if he was on the prison yard.

The two came out here every Sunday to chop it up and spend some father and son time since they both had busy lives.

Boss hit a three-point range shot winning the last game. Boss won four games and Ty won two games, but he was far from tired thanks to hours of burpees he used to do in the pen.

"Good game, son. How's your mom and brother?" Ty asked, taking a towel wiping the sweat off his chest and drinking water.

"My mom's good, I told her you were out she was glad for you. She be working and going on trips all over the place. As for my little bro, I don't really talk to him as much," Boss stated honestly, sitting down, catching his breath, and getting dressed in his Angel Palm's sweatsuit.

"I understand but he's still your blood and at the end of the day you'll be surprised how far blood will go for you when blood is spilled."

"Facts."

"Speaking of blood, I've been meaning to tell you something. I ran into a woman I was dealing with recently and she told me I had a daughter. Crazy right?"

"Damn, pops, you was getting busy."

"Yeah, I'm not proud of that, son. That's how I lost your mother, but I took a DNA and the girl is mine. So, you got a sister out there somewhere. I didn't even meet her because her mother think I should just leave things how they are," Ty said.

"You going for that?"

"I'ma think of something."

"Good because I want to meet her."

"Me too, but how's the car lot going? I'm so glad you're not out here in these streets. It's dangerous out here and different from how it used to be," Ty said as two older women walked past them waving at him.

"The lot's doing good, it's a success and hard work," Boss stated.

"Good, continue doing good."

"I gotta go, I'ma see you next Sunday. I love you," Boss hugged his dad.

"I love you, too," Ty said, getting dressed.

***

Westside, Chi-Town

Boss leaned back in the Cadillac CTS-V watching a gang of little niggas run up to the BMW X5M handing the driver money. Boss knew whoever the driver was, he had to just receive over 70k in sixty seconds. He saw a little GD kid walking past his car toward the BMW counting money. Boss blew his horn getting the big head kid's attention who rocked a black flag on his head.

"What's good folk?" Boss said as the young teen looked through the tints that were halfway down.

"You, GD?" the kid asked

"Facts," Boss threw up a folk sign.

"A'ight, I thought you were an op homie. I was about to drill you," the kid said, lifting his long black T-shirt, showing a Tech 9 machine gun.

"Who runs this block now that Trey's gone?" Boss asked.

"Man, this shit crazy because you see that BMW up the street, he took over. He's a Stone them niggas we never allowed over here but everybody knows he killed Trey and they don't want no smoke. He be having his people off the block running down on niggas, shooting niggas, they just killed Romo last night because he lost his pack."

"What's the dude's name in the truck?" Boss asked.

"He calls himself S.Man. He got some coke that got fiends going crazy. He always got three shooters with him with Dracos ready to drill shit."

"A'ight homie, good looking. This for you," Boss said handing the kid 3,000 before pulling off with everything he needed to put a master plan together.

Romell Tukes

Chapter 13

Downtown, Chi-Town

Boss finished placing an order for a shipment of new luxury cars mostly Audis and Porsches because they were selling very fast on his lot. He'd been so busy with work and hunting down S. Man he hadn't been making time for his wife. Last night was the first time in weeks he and Rosie made love. They were drained and tired in minutes because of their busy schedules.

The good news was Malik would be home soon and he'd found a location on S. Man. He had Animal people run S. Man's license plate on his BMW. The name that popped up was a Tian Martin who lived in Harvey, IL on Maple Ave.

Boss figured that had to be his wife or a close family member of his. So, he made plans to pay Tian a visit soon, but first, he sent C. Boy and his crew to rob all of S. Man's spots. S. Man led him to all his stash spots the other day as he tailed him close for almost eight hours.

Boss realized it was past 9 p.m. so he grabbed his Hermes coat and made his way out of his office, so he could meet C. Boy before he went home.

Boss locked his car dealership and climbed in his Wraith feeling the cold fall wind almost knock his hat off. He pulled out onto the main entrance to see a black SUV coming down the street. He put on his right blinker letting the truck pass and it slowed down. The truck made a complete stop in front of the Wraith. Boss blew his horn so the driver behind the tints could move.

The passenger and back doors flew open, Boss saw Face and B. Stone hop out with AK 47s firing into the Wraith.

Rah! Tat! Tat! Tat! Tat! Tat! Tat! Tat! Tat!

Boss put the Wraith in reverse and hit the gas backing up, hitting a Lexus.

"Shit!" Boss yelled as bullets weaved past his head, shattering his windows. It was a miracle he didn't get hit once

When he made it to another entrance he raced onto the streets as the SUV was closing on him.

Boss hit the gas swerving past an 18-wheeler looking in his rearview mirror to see the SUV still on him. Boss busted a left on to the expressway, dipping in and out of traffic until he jumped off the near exit. Face was sixty feet behind him. Boss ran two red lights on a main street almost causing a big accident and he hopped on another expressway losing them. Boss was mad he got caught slipping by two old ass niggas, he hated that he had to run and play cat and mice, but he had no choice.

He got off the exit on the Westside to meet C. Boy, but first, he had to get rid of the Wraith he loved. There were so many holes in the Wraith it looked like the army used the car for target practice.

C. Boy had some people who had a chop shop, so he planned to take it there and cop something new in the morning.

***

Days Later

C. Boy was dressed up like a fiend as he walked through an alley in the Village area where Smitty's traps were.

"Yo' what you trying to get? a tall nigga said posted up with two of his homies drinking and serving fiends as they did all night.

"Two dimes of hard," C. Boy said with a slow walk.

"These base heads love this shit," the tall dude turned around to go inside the trash can where he hid his work just in case the police jumped out on the block as they normally did.

Boc! Boc! Boc! Boc! Boc!

C. Boy shot two of the hustlers in the neck. By the time the tall dude came out of the trash C. Boy had his Draco to the back of his head.

"Where is S. Man's trap house?"

"Man, who the fuck is S. Man?"

"Nigga, don't play with me," C. Boy said pressing the Draco barrel harder against his head.

"There is no S. Man over here, bro. I swear on my seeds, Joe, please don't kill me."

"Who runs this hood?"

"Smitty."

"Where his trap house?"

"Right there, through that back yard with the wood wall and those Beware signs."

"Good looking, Joe," C. Boy said before blowing his brains into the garbage can as he made his way through the backyard to hear loud music blasting from inside the house.

C. Boy tried to open the back door, but it was locked. He saw four young niggas in the living room yelling, drinking, and watching G-Herb video on a 72-inch flat-screen TV.

Just as luck was on his side, one of the young nigga opened the door, and C. Boy hid on the side of the wall. The young nigga looked no older than sixteen as he stepped out to use his cell phone because it was too late inside.

When he turned around because he thought he heard a sound he was face to face with a gun he saw too often.

"How many inside?" C. Boy asked.

"Three," the kid said nervously

"Where's Smitty's stash?"

"My uncle hides it inside the couch."

"Take me inside," C. Boy said, turning him around, leading him inside with the gun in his lower back.

"Damn, Spice, who called you wifey? I been trying to hit that for years," Pig said when he saw Spice come back inside with a crazy look on his face as he stood in the doorway.

"You good, bro?" Baby Stone said who was sitting at the living room table busting down two keys as the loud music filled the house.

Boc! Boc!

C. Boy shot Spice in his back then he popped out from behind firing two more shots in Pig's head.

Baby Stone reached for his Glock 17 to only be shot four times in his chest. The last kid tried to run out of the front door until C.

Boy's bullets hawked him down and six shots entered his lower back, dropping him in the doorway.

C. Boy lifted the couch to see two full duffle bags full of money. He took them and left out the back door. His car was parked up the block where three of his guys were waiting for him and watching his back. C. Boy loved to put in work alone. He thought that made a savage instead of doing dirt with ten niggas who would eventually snitch on a nigga if in a jam.

***

Harvey, IL

Tian was in her house getting ready to take her twin daughters trick or treating around the middle-class neighborhood. Tian was a forty-year-old, dark-skinned, chubby woman with a cute face, and green eyes. She'd been married to Smitty forever, they were soulmates since teens. She couldn't see her life being with someone else.

She knew her husband cheated from time to time, but he was a man. She used to see her pops do it to her mother daily. In recent years since having children, Tian put on more than eighty pounds due to stress eating and sitting home being a housewife and mother.

She used to be one of the baddest bitches in her hood until getting married and having kids.

While Smitty ran the streets, she took care of the house and kids, it wasn't her plan growing up because she had dreams to be a singer.

"Mommy, how do I look?" little Taleka said running into her mom's room dressed as Superwoman. Her twin sister came behind her dressed as Poison Ivy.

"You two look so cute," Tian looked at her beautiful daughters as the doorbell rang.

Trick or Treaters had been coming all day to get candy as kids went house to house for Halloween.

"Come on, it's time for us to go anyway," Tian said walking downstairs to see a kid dressed in a Jason X outfit for Halloween.

Tian grabbed the bowl of candy by the door.

"Mommy, let me give out the candy," one of the twins said.

Tian handed her the bowl full of candy before she opened the door.

"Trick or treat," the kid said with a bag in his left hand and a gun in his other.

"Mommy, his outfit is cool. Look at the water gun." Taleka was excited.

"Cute, I don't ever remember Jason carrying a gun. But ain't you too old to be trick or treating?" Tian said looking at how tall he was.

The kid laughed before he raised the gun shooting Tian in her head, the twins screamed before Animal silenced them for life with bullets. Animal then took the bowl of candy off the floor and walked down the street full of kids. Animal had a silencer attached to his Ruger so nobody would hear the gruesome killing.

"Where you get the candy from?" Boss said sitting inside the driver's seat of a Ford Focus as Animal hopped in the car.

"I've never been trick or treating," Animal said, eating a mini kit-kat candy.

Boss pulled off seeing kids running up and down the street dressed in their Halloween attire.

Romell Tukes

Chapter 14

Cook County Jail

"I'm fucking free bitches!" Malik yelled as he walked out of the jail as a free man, dressed in a Burberry sweatsuit Boss had sent him.

Malik heard loud bangs on the jail windows as inmates showed him love and he threw up his Vice Lord gang sign before walking into the parking lot. He saw Boss leaning on an all-white, new Maybach and Animal leaning on a new, lime green Lamborghini Aventador.

"Welcome home, bro." Boss hugged Malik, their bond went from strong to unbreakable in the last year.

"Thanks, I can't believe how that trial shit went down," Malik said.

"Don't forget I'm here," Animal said

"Animal, good to see you," Malik stated as the two dapped each other up and Animal saw that he'd cut his dreads.

"These whips is like that, Joe, y'all niggas doing numbers," Malik said.

Boss laughed. "Nigga this Maybach yours. I got the Rolls Royce Coupe after ops turned my shit into swiss cheese," Boss said.

Malik admired the pearl-white Maybach feeling like the king he was. "What ops?" Malik asked.

Animal laughed. "I gotta make a move across town so I'ma slide on y'all late.," Animal hopped in his Lambo and swerved off.

"What's up with him, he still on some funny shit?" Malik asked, getting into the driver's seat of the widebody with dark curtains.

"You know how he is, bro. But he's the reason why you out, bro," Boss said as they saw a couple of female C.O.s staring at them with lust.

"Yo', Mrs. Jenkins, what's up?" Malik popped his head out of his car.

"Malik, that's you? Damn, boy, I see you doing it big," she said showing her beautiful smile on her way to work a double.

"I'm not doing it big until I got you."

"Boy, you gonna need more than a Maybach to slide in this wetness," Mrs. Jenkins said, her girlfriend laughed and so did Boss.

"I guess I gotta get the Wraith?"

"More like a private jet," she said walking off, her ass hugged her work pants.

"Damn, that bitch bad with her high-yellow, thick ass. She used to dance at Ace of Spade." Malik drove off.

"I gotta fill you in on what's going on, but we can do that later. I got a surprise for you, drive to Clyde street," Boss said.

Malik played some music by his favorite rapper, Lil Durk, on the touch screen installed system.

***

107 Champlain

Lil BD and Hitler were on Hitler's block full of Four Corner Hustlers selling drugs in the cold and throwing bricks at police cars then running.

"Where you been, bro?" Hitler said sipping lean out of a foam cup, sitting on the hood of his Audi RS7.

"Shit crazy, right now, bro. I been meaning to get at you but first I had to figure some shit out."

"What's up? It's time to slide on some goofies," Hitler said with a slur in his voice.

"I don't know yet, bro, because this is too close to home. You remember them Chi' Raq Gangsta niggas?" Lil BD asked.

"Who don't? They still got the whole city after them, bro. They killed a lot of powerful niggas. They killed my big homie, Lil Moe, if I ever catch them niggas it's lit. But I heard one of them niggas just beat two cop bodies," Hitler said.

"I heard."

"What's up with them, though? I heard them niggas is ghost," Hitler said.

"Nah, I know who they are."

"What!" Hitler said ready to ride. "Let's go, we out. I been waiting for this day!" Hitler said getting hyped.

"It's not that easy."

"Why?"

"Because it's, Boss."

"Boss who nigga?" Hitler shouted

"Nigga, my brother."

"Are you sure? That shit's crazy, my nigga. What the fuck you want to do homie?"

"I don't know yet but if we push, we gotta push hard because you know how they get down."

"I'ma always go hard for mines," Hitler said tapping the twin Desert Eagles on his hips.

"When I figure it out I'ma holler at you."

"A'ight. You trying to hit up Adreana tonight or Sky-11?" Hitler said feeling in a club mode.

"It don't matter, call Force and Bow Bow so all the guys can come out tonight. It's Force G Day," Lil BD said and Hitler called Force.

***

Downtown, Chi-Town

Simone walked through the Lincoln Mall on her way to the food court to see her cousin who'd hit her up on her Facebook messenger. Whom she hadn't seen in over a year or two. She wore a white DKNY dress with heels and a fur coat while her Prada sunglasses gave her night-time vision. Simone walked through the food court looking for her cousin but didn't see him.

"Simone!" a voice said to the side of her, it was a man reading a newspaper wearing sunglasses and a hoodie as if he was hiding.

"Face!" she yelled

"Shhhh, sit down," Face said

"Oh, my God you look different. Why are you trying to hide?" she asked suspiciously.

"Listen to me, last year I was kidnapped and almost killed but luckily I got away," he said.

"That's why I haven't seen you. Have you heard what happened to Tian and the kids on Halloween?" she asked, remembering seeing it on the news before her cousin called her crying.

"I know they killed my family, Simone," Face said in a painful voice.

"Who, Face? We can go to the police."

"No, we don't move like that, Simone. I will handle this shit, but have you seen Malik?" he asked.

She looked at him awkwardly wondering why he wanted to know where her boo was.

"No, I haven't seen him yet. Why?"

"He's the one who kidnapped me with his crew, Simone. He killed my family."

"Face you tripping, he was in jail when Tian died. He called me from jail that day," she defended Malik.

"Simone, listen to me he is a Chi' Raq Gangsta he and his crew got a lot of people after him." The name Chi Raq Gangstas rang a bell in her head. She couldn't remember where she'd heard that name from. "I need you to bring him to me or just call me when he gets around you," Face requested.

"Nigga, you lost your damn mind? I ain't about to set up my nigga. You got me fucked up," Simone said getting up to leave.

"You walk away, Simone, you become an op with him."

"Suck a dick," she said walking away upset.

Chapter 15

Southside, Chi-Town

King Mike and King Papi waited in the Rite Aid parking lot on 26th California Street a well-known Latin King turf ran by King Papi

"I've been hearing a lot of good things about this dude." King Papi was smoking a blunt full of exotic weed looking out the windows of Vegas' Yellow Lexus RCF waiting for Boss.

"Boss is a cash cow and he good people and he's married to Rosie," King Mike said, seeing a Rolls Royce Dawn pull into the lot.

"Rosie got married? Damn, she's always been beautiful, top five in the city. I went to school with her when I came out here from the Bronx, she had everybody going crazy," King Papi said in his New York accent.

King Papi was a twenty-four-year-old self-made killer with a bag. He was King Mike's right-hand man since he came to Chi-Town from New York to live with his pops who was also a Latin King.

"He went to the same school as Rosie dumb nigga. Oh, I forgot you got kicked out of the 7th grade, did a bid, and never went back," King Mike said flashing his lights.

"Shit happens, King."

"Come on and stop talking please you get beside yourself," King Mike said hopping out in his Saint Laurent outfit with his two Cuban Link chains swinging

"King Mike, what's good, Joe? I see you shining in them VVS diamonds," Boss said embracing his plug.

"Only at night, I see you went and outdid yourself," King Mike said looking at the Rolls Royce Dawn Coupe.

"Sumthin' light, next it's the Lambo truck. But what's going on?" Boss said looking at the young man standing next to him with the long hair and scar on the left side of his face.

"This my fam, King Papi, he's my right hand. I'ma be in Puerto Rico for a couple of weeks with my plug and people, so he's going to be handling all my business affairs."

"What's good, bro?" King Papi said.

Boss nodded, he only liked dealing with the plug and no middle man because that was most niggas downfall in the game when the Feds came out to play.

"We still set for tonight?" Boss asked.

"Yep, your shit should be at the regular location in twenty-seven minutes," King Mike said looking at his big face Audemars Piguet white gold watch.

"A'ight, I'ma give you a call when everything is set. King Papi nice meeting you. Whenever King Mike leaves holler at me so we can link up," Boss said.

"I got you folk," King Papi stated before he and his big homie climbed in the Lexus and pulled off to go attend to other businesses across town.

***

Chicago Heights

Beacon Hill was a dangerous area full of drugs, violence, and prostitution by women of all ages. This area was Smitty and Ty's turf; it was a goldmine area clocking in 120K a day off hand to hand. It was 8:00 a.m. and niggas were out trapping because in the morning dope fiends came out to get their morning wake-up hit.

"The block is crazy this morning," Mookie said as he approached his crew posted on the brick wall, counting the money they made in the last hour.

"Yo', Stone, what's good with that eater I saw you with last night? You couldn't put the homies on? What happened to bros before hoes?" Mookie said tucking $1850 in his Balmain jean pockets.

"That's what I said when you cuffed Jessica," Stone said talking about Mookie's girlfriend that the gang wanted to fuck but Mookie was cuffing her because her pussy was on another level.

"Fuck I look like letting the gang hit it before I do?" Mookie said in his defense.

The crew saw a Jeep Wrangler, all-black pull up on them with tints and they all reached for their poles.

"Y'all know them niggas, Joe?" Mookie asked his Black P Stones homies.

Before anyone could reply C. Boy and Boss hopped out with masks on and RPG assault rifles, firing rounds, they scattered but didn't make it far.

Tat! Tat! Tat! Tat! Tat! Tat! Tat! Tat! Tat! Tat!

Civilians across the street heard the loud commotion and took off running down the street screaming.

Boss ran down on Mookie who was on his back next to three dead bodies in a pool of blood.

"Nigga, where you going?" Boss said pointing the big assault rifle only used in the military at his head.

C. Boy and Boss saw all six men dead as they ran to the Jeep and raced off driving wildly, they heard sirens three blocks down in their rearview mirrors.

Boss had been watching the six men since they arrived on the block hours ago, he waited until the traffic slowed down because fiends normally had lines wrapped around the block to be served. He knew Smitty was moving weight on this block because he'd followed him here twice a day with his entourage that he kept 24/7.

"That was close," C. Boy said on the expressway, his adrenaline was rushing through his veins.

"Yeah, we good, bro. That was good work back there. Now I know why Trey spoke so highly of you," Boss stated, making C. Boy feel special.

"Gotta play for keeps in the field, bro," C. Boy said as they got stuck in the morning traffic.

***

Next Day

"You gotta be fucking with me, Smitty? First, it was four of your guys, your family, and now six of the little homies?" Ty shouted pissed off as they talked in a hotel parking lot where Smitty was staying since he'd lost his wife and kids.

"Whoever we're up against, Ty, we need to stop them before they get us next. Do you know how it feels to bury your daughters and wife at the same time?" Smitty said emotionally with pain and grief on his face.

"We gonna figure this shit out, but I want you to find out who Trey had ties to. And what's the name of that crew you said was out here turning the city up a few years ago?" Ty asked.

"The Chi'Raq Gangstas."

"Yeah, look into them because whoever coming for us, they're professionals," Ty said.

Smitty nodded his head before turning to leave.

"I love you, bro," Ty said.

Smitty stopped. "Love just got my family killed," Smitty said coldly before walking off.

Ty climbed in his Mercedes and pulled off in deep thought about the recent events. He made Smitty keep guards with him because he knew whoever was lurking was on to Smitty's movements, so his life was at risk.

As he was driving through Downtown, Ty was unaware of the black Audi TLX sedan that had been following him for over two weeks.

***

Cook County Jail

Ra Ra walked out of the jail gates in the same clothes he came to jail in which was Old Navy jeans and an American Eagle T-shirt.

It was so cold outside his balls were already numb and his toes in his dirty white Air Force Ones sneakers were frozen.

Ra Ra was going to stay with his sister in South Chi-Town; that was the only place he had to go besides a homeless shelter. Since his old celly Malik went home he'd been sending Ra Ra money, pics, and having chicks bring him drugs into the jail. He was leaving with 11,500 on a debit card, he planned to go shopping and get a pack so he could get on his feet.

When he made it to the bus stop, he saw a cute Spanish chick sitting there with headphones in her ears. He was about to say something until he saw her look him up and down with a disgusted look as if she prayed, he didn't even look at her.

Ra Ra just stood there and waited for the bus, then he saw a mean red Camaro slowly drive down the block outside of the jail with tints. Ra Ra thought a nigga was about to do a drill, so he stood his ground.

When the Camaro came to a full stop, the door opened and Malik stepped out with a Balenciaga bag and car keys.

"What's up, bro?" Ra Ra smiled and hugged Malik as if he was a long, lost brother.

"Here take that shit off and put this on." Malik passed him a Balenciaga hoodie and jeans with the Balenciaga boots.

Ra Ra got dressed right in the middle of the road stripping down to his boxers and tank top.

"Good looking, bro, this shit fly and new," Ra Ra said looking inside the clean car with the red and black racing seats. He used to always talk Malik's head off at night about Camaros.

"This is yours, nigga. I don't drive muscle cars, Joe,," Malik handed him the car keys.

The Spanish chick waiting at the bus stop watched both men closely.

"Thanks, bro, I can't believe this," Ra Ra said as he hopped inside.

Malik smiled, it felt good doing for him what his homie did for him when he came home.

Ra Ra pulled a U-turn and stopped in front of the bus stop, the Spanish chick took out her headphones, smiling hard showing her gap and yellow teeth.

"You need a ride?" Ra Ra said.

"Yeah," she said.

"You better ride a dick, bitch!" Ra Ra yelled, he saw her get up with her bag before he pulled off.

"Mrs. Jenkins was talking to the inmates about how you pulled out in a Maybach. She told niggas they needed to be like you."

"That's nothing, bro, you with me now. I'ma make you rich."

Chapter 16

Downtown, Chi-Town

Malik had his face buried in Simone's phat, red, bald pussy as he sucked her clit.

"Ooohhh, yesss, Malik!" She grinded her hips into his face as his lips massaged her thin pretty pussy lips.

"You miss me?" he said sliding two fingers into her gushy waterfall.

She went crazy. "I'm cumming, Malik! Do that shit, daddy," she moaned and began shaking as cream squirted on his tongue.

Malik continued to nip nibble lightly on her swollen clit and she grabbed his head and rode his face.

"Suck that pussy, daddy! Ohhhh, oh my fucking god!" she yelled, climaxing and feeling her legs lock up on her.

"You good?" Malik said whipping the semen off his mouth, she looked exhausted.

"Fuck yeah, now fuck me from the back. Then I want to finally try the backdoor," she said bending over spreading her nice, big, round ass.

"You sure?"

"Yeah, baby, just be easy on me. Okay?"

Malik entered her pussy which was wet but extra tight, it took him a couple of strokes to loosen her up.

"Damnnn, fuck me," she moaned as he spread her ass cheeks looking into her tiny, brown hole that looked closed.

Malik was deep in her pussy as she bounced up and down on his dick feeling him touch her G-spot while she grabbed the headboard and forced her force on his dick.

"Take this dick," Malik moaned as her pussy muscles clutched his dick and he gripped her ass cheeks.

"I'm about to cum on your dick! Fuck me harder!" she yelled as he started pounding out her pussy with all the force his core would allow to. She arched her back so he could go deeper into her guts and she came on his dick.

Malik did something he wasn't used to, he dived his face into her asshole and ate her ass, which shocked her.

"Ohhhhh, shittt, nigga!" she yelled making sex faces and biting her bottom lip.

When he was done eating her ass it was sloppy wet and he slowly entered her tiny brown hole making her leap forward

"Take your time, mmm."

Malik had the tip of his dick inside, he grabbed her waist and slowly thrust into her.

"I—I—I—can't!" she yelled when he was halfway in ripping her asshole open.

"Just relax, boo. I got you," Malik assured as he went slowly in, hearing her moans and cries of pleasure.

Simone squeezed tightly as he went deeper into her lower back.

"Ugghhhh, I love it!" she screamed, slowly throwing her ass back on him, making him go deeper.

He grabbed her long hair. Seconds later, she was riding his dick like a pony taking his whole pipe in and out of her ass until he came in her.

"That was amazing," Simone said as they cuddled both outta breathe as if they'd just run 50 laps.

"It's amazing, I'm just glad to be home."

"Me too, I had to cry myself to sleep every night," Simone said honestly.

"I'm sorry, it will never happen again."

"It better not, but I went to meet with my cousin Face at the mall a couple of weeks ago. He told me you kidnapped him and killed my little cousins. I know that was a lie because you was still in jail on that day," she said, looking into his sexy eyes to see if she saw any truthfulness to what Face told her.

"What! Is he fucking crazy?" Malik said pissed that he told Simone about the kidnapping.

"He then told me you were part of the Chi'Raq Gangstas. I asked someone about them. I heard they're dangerous people, but I know you not that type of person. Face told me to set you up and I cursed his ass out. I would never cross you like that, I love you," she said.

"I love you, too! Don't worry about him. Let's do round three."

"I know what you need," she said, lowering herself to his dick and began sucking and slurping like Roxy Reynolds or Mya G.

***

Harvey, IL

The neighborhood Bossville was nicknamed Crackville since Boss took over the whole hood. Boss had over ten traps and six stash houses within blocks of each other just so his workers could keep an eye on the drugs and money.

Smitty and a three-man crew all sat on the corner of the block in a black Honda CR-V watching a couple of Boss' workers sell drugs hand to hand in front of a tall brick building with a two-way entrance. Smitty counted five more hoodlums coming out of the building with the other five Gangsta Disciples posted up.

Smitty found out Trey was working for a kid named Boss whose name Smitty had been hearing for a while. He wasn't 100% sure he was the one who killed his family, but he was going to find out.

When he did his research on the Chi' Raq Gangstas he came up short, the only thing he came up with was a Vice Lord named Malik who'd just come home from being acquitted for killing two police.

Smitty was connected so when he asked about Boss traps, he got an address to two places minutes away from each other. He planned to kill two birds with one stone tonight.

"It's time." Smitty cocked his pistol and everybody else did the same before hopping out.

A couple of GDs was standing outside, the rest were in the lobby building, trying to stay warm tonight because it was under 30 degrees

Smitty and his crew crept toward the front of the building, when one of the GDs saw Smitty, he pulled out and shot one of the gunmen in the chest. Shit went crazy after that, shots were fired from inside the building but Smitty and his now two men crew were taking the GDs out back to back.

When Smitty saw that everybody was dead he left stepping over the dead body of his soldier as if he wasn't even there.

***

Smitty pulled up in front of some old-boarded row houses, to see a gang of GDs all with black flags on their head, enjoying the night as if it was summertime on the block. There were two young girls outside they were fifteen-years-old acting eighteen, so they could slide with one of the hustlers tonight instead of going home to their crackhead mothers.

"Y'all just sit back and watch this shit," Smitty said looking across the street as he hopped out of the Honda to hear the crew of kids laughing and yelling.

Smitty popped the trunk and grabbed the heavy Rocket Launcher he'd had for years but never used. When he placed it over his shoulder, one of the drug dealers pointed at the big man across the street, when he shot off the rocket launcher everybody took off, but it was too late.

Boom!

The explosion killed 12 people and blew up three cars and two abandoned homes. The block looked like a wildfire, Smitty dipped off in the Honda laughing, his two goons was scared to death.

Chapter 17

Downtown, Chi-Town

Ace Gentlemen's club was popping with the hottest strippers in the city only ballers and self-made niggas were allowed in the upscale club. The club had two-floor levels with five VIP sections on each floor, two bars, private rooms to fuck in if a nigga could afford it, and private show booths.

"This shit on another level," Ra Ra said as he watched two sexy, redbone dancers with tats all over their bodies, kissing each other on stage. Niggas was deep in the crowd with money and guns turning up as the two bitches climbed up the pole with one hand doing tricks.

"I never been in this bitch," Malik pulled a bottle of Deuces out of the ice bucket.

"Did you holler at the guys to see if I can get down?" Ra Ra stressed the fact that he was trying to be a part of the famous Chi'Raq Gangstas.

"Yeah, you part of the fam, bro. I told you that, little homie," Malik said watching the crowd because it was too many niggas in the spot.

He looked out of the dark VIP section as the lights danced around the club. The sounds of FDG Duck song had the dancers twerking upside down as the club was going crazy, they saw the women's pretty, high yellow pussies.

"A'ight, good. When we going on some missions?" Ra Ra said as a slim, brown skin, cute chick approached their section, dressed in high heels and thongs with nice, perky C-cup titties out.

"So, just be patient."

"Hey, what's up, handsome?" the dancer they called Yandy asked Ra Ra. She was six-inches taller as he looked up.

"You tell me," Ra Ra said, catching her vibe and noticing her staring at her phat puss that was nearly busting out of her thongs.

"You tryna go somewhere private if you can afford my time?" she said, brushing her long hair to the side.

She rocked Rihanna's hairdo with half her head shaved but she looked cut with it, unlike most women.

"I'll be back," Ra Ra said standing up to leave.

"Handle your business, Lord," Malik laughed. He knew she was about to break his little ass with her spider legs.

Malik planned to take Ra Ra with him to look for Smitty who was becoming a big problem. Boss filled him in on everything that was going on. He was ready to put in some work. He regained his blocks that Boss was holding down for him in Chicago Heights. He knew Ra Ra could be a big help, so Boss agreed. Animal, on the other hand, was against it, he'd been putting Ra Ra down a lot lately.

***

Riverdale, IL

Face exited his baby mother's complex after spending time with a couple of his kids. Now he was on his way to East St. Louis to check his other baby mothers and kids. He had four baby mothers and so many kids he would forget their names. After he came from St. Louis, he had to holler at B. Stone to take care of this Boss's situation, he was going crazy especially after he killed his kids. Face hit the alarm button to his bulletproof Callaway Tahoe SUV, he saw a shadow behind which made him turn around to a taser to his neck and his body crashed onto the floor, shaking.

Animal grabbed his hoodie and started dragging him. Face screamed until he hit him with the taser again for a total of twenty seconds, almost killing him. Boss pulled up in the minivan, Animal tossed his body inside before climbing inside. Once inside Animal tied Face up and duct-taped his mouth, as Boss drove away at normal speed through the quiet dark neighborhood.

***

Southside, Chi-Town

Face woke up to see Boss and Animal standing over him smiling, Face looked around seeing that he was in a familiar setting. When he got his vision back, he realized he was in the same basement he'd been in two years ago when he was kidnapped by the same niggas.

"You're crazy if you think I'ma let you get away this time, Joe." Animal sat down on a large container.

"You're both dead men, I swear all of you. I already exposed you all. Everybody gonna know who the Chi'Raq Gangstas is," Face said in tears thinking about how they did his kids and what he had coming.

"You done?" Boss said grabbing an ax and a chainsaw off the wooden table on its last leg about to tip over. "Which one you think, Animal?" Boss asked.

"Axe, the chainsaw takes too long," Animal said smiling, looking at Face's stretched out body.

"Just shoot me, bitch nigga! Who you think you are?" Face said looking at the ax swinging in his hand.

"Which hand you roll with?" Boss asked making Animal laugh remembering that scene from *Belly*.

"Why?" Face said.

Boss was now kneeling on his arm then he swung the Axe and chopped off his left hand.

"Ahhhhhh!" Face yelled in pain.

"I can't hear you now! I'ma bitch nigga," Boss said grabbing his leg, chopping off his foot.

"Mamaaaaa ahhh!" he yelled before he passed out and lost consciousness due to the loss of blood.

Boss began cutting off all his lambs, the ax was so sharp it only took one swing to slice through his flesh.

"Damn, Boss," Animal said, chopping off his neck.

Face's head rolled off his shoulders. After twenty minutes of dismantling his body, it was time for Animal to work his magic. Animal put on a face mask, long gloves, and goggles, and took the lid off the metal container he was sitting on, seeing smoke raise.

The acid chemical in the container was to take the flesh off Face's bones to take away any prints or DNA that could lead back to them.

As Animal started tossing Face's body parts into the container Boss just watched, wondering where he'd come up with the acid idea.

"We gotta let this shit sit overnight." Animal tossed Face's foot in the acid, hearing it sizzle.

"A'ight, cool, I'm out," Boss said, looking at the blood all over his black Champion sweatsuit.

***

Roseland Strip Mall: Days Later

Simone arrived from shopping in her favorite Chanel store in the mall. She had lunch plans with Malik at a nice, upscale restaurant downtown in a couple of minutes. It was a nice day outside with spring right around the corner, the winter was starting to break.

She was walking to her Lexus LC Coupe that Malik had recently got her. The recent death of Face was big news to her family. The murder was so brutal it would make anyone's stomach turn. The police found Face's body parts in an acid container in the city garbage station. At first, he was a John Doe until they used his Dental records to identify his body.

She had a clue it could've been Malik from what she told him, but she didn't ask him and didn't plan to. As she got to her car, someone grabbed her by the neck and started choking her with chicken wire, it cut through her neck and blood squirted out.

Simone couldn't even put up a fight, then the wire sliced her neck wide open, killing her.

B. Stone watched her lifeless body slump on her car door. He took off his gloves and slowly walked off to his Benz truck a couple of cars down. He was told to kill her before Face's body parts were found because Face told him she was an op, he was waiting for the perfect time. Now he planned to hunt Malik because he knew his crew was responsible for his friend's murder.

"Ohhh, my God, someone call the police!" an old, white woman yelled.

B. Stone pulled off watching the civilians surround Simone's dead body.

Romell Tukes

Chapter 18

University of Chicago

Today was Jenny's college graduation, she sat in the crowd of students in a purple gown and hat as the college professors gave long-ass speeches. She was so happy to receive her degree she'd worked so hard for. When she heard her name to go up to the stage to receive her degrees, she jumped up. Jenny heard Lil BD yelling her name and a couple of her classmates, as she snatched her diploma from the white, racist professor who she disliked.

As the ceremony finished everybody was happy and excited, and talking about their future careers. Jenny saw Lil BD walking toward her in a white Louis Vuitton suit looking like a GQ model with his waves spinning.

"Baby, I did it!" Jenny hugged him then kissed his soft lips.

"You did congratulations," Lil BD said admiring how beautiful she looked with little make-up and her long hair hanging down her backside.

"Let's get up outta here," Jenny said and they walked through the grass to the student parking lot.

"Thank you for coming, babe, I'm so happy."

"You never have to thank me for doing what I'm supposed to do."

"I know but you know what I mean, love," she said seeing a letter and three thick brown envelopes on her driver's seat. "Who the fuck?" she said not realizing her car door was unlocked.

Lil BD thought something was wrong when he saw her reaction, then he saw the brown envelopes which looked like money. He wanted to question her as she started reading the card.

When Jenny read the card, she had tears in her eyes.

"You okay?" he asked.

She didn't answer, Jenny hopped in her Porsche Cayenne truck and tossed the envelopes full of money and the card out the window.

"I'll meet you at home," she said before pulling off in tears.

Lil BD picked up the money and counted it there was 100,000 in each envelope. He read the card by the anonymous person, then stopped halfway and ripped it up before leaving.

***

Downtown, Chi-Town: Weeks Later

Smitty was chilling in his hotel room where he'd been for the past couple of months until he killed his ops and found a new place to rest his head. It was too dangerous for him to look for a home now because Boss was still out there.

Ty told him he thought it was a bad idea for him to live at a hotel but Smitty told him it was his best bet because nobody would think to get at a nigga in a hotel.

He kept three goons in the next two rooms on standby just in case some shit was to pop off. Smitty rarely left the room unless he was tailing Boss or walking to the gas station behind the hotel for some Newport 100's cigarettes. Due to the war, the drug profit had gone down 17% because Boss and his people were hitting his spots and killing his men. Smitty looked at the clock to see that it was 1:42 a.m. He reached for his pack of cigarettes.

"Damn!" he shouted outta cigarettes.

He knew he would have to go to the store because his little soldiers didn't smoke. Luckily the gas station was open around the clock.

Smitty threw on his XL Gucci sweatsuit made for big niggas and a pair of AGG Nike bootz. Smitty grabbed his .380 special handgun and his 9mm pistol before leaving his room. He took the back way which was shorter and there were no street lights, a person could see the gas station a block away.

Smitty saw a stray dog digging in the trash. "Fucking bum," he said to himself hearing another noise to his right which made him pull his 9mm out.

Ra Ra stepped out from the side of the wall with a pistol pointed at him.

"Drop it," Smitty said

"Nigga, you drop it," Ra Ra replied.

Both men stared at each other.

"You think you creeping on an OG, nigga? Y'all little niggas just started drilling. I'ma give you three seconds. One—two—" Smitty counted down seeing no fear in Ra Ra's eyes.

"—three—nigga drop it," a voice said behind Smitty holding a 50 Caliber canon to the back of his head catching him lacking.

"A'ight, young blood, you got me." Smitty dropped his gun and lifted his hands. He was upset that he fell for the oldest trick in the book.

"So, you the damn nigga who's been getting at us? Well, I'm here now. I just want to know who sent you?" Malik said

"Does it matter? I tell you it won't be long before y'all luck comes to a dry spell," Smitty said looking at Ra Ra knowing him from his old neighborhood.

"You're right.

Boom! Boom!

Malik blew his head off and Ra Ra shot Smitty seven times in the stomach for good measure.

***

Buff City

Lil BD was riding around in his BMW i8 with his homie PG who'd just come home from doing a three-year prison bid for selling drugs.

"Glad you home, bro. A lot of shit has changed, the guys is on money now, folk," Lil BD said driving through the block, seeing his own homie ice grilling him with envy.

Lil BD knew he had haters in his own hood but he didn't care as long as they stayed in their lane because it was nothing for him to drop a bag on a nigga's head to get rid of him.

"I been hearing, bro. Your name is going crazy behind the wall. Everybody on your dick in Statesville, bro," PG said smiling and showing his chipped tooth.

PG was a BD under Loso, he was skinny, tall, with a fade haircut, big eyes, big lips, and thick bushy eyebrows. He'd been a shooter since a young kid. He and Lil BD were close, they even put in work a couple of times for Loso together.

"I be sending money and bitches up there with some dope and crystal for the guys. I tried to set you up, but when you told me you was touching soon, I knew what time it was." Lil BD stopped at a red light.

"Yeah, three-k a month was more than enough for me from you. I appreciate that," PG said seriously

"That's nothing, bro. Now it's time to focus on these streets," Lil BD stated.

"Facts, but first I need to take care of these niggas who killed my pops."

"Oh, yeah, I heard about that."

"Yeah, my dad wasn't an angel, but Premium changed his life. He was the deacon of the church and gave his life to God," PG said thinking back to when he got the news from the prison Chaplin that his father was shot in the head and found dead in his car.

"I'm with you, bro, me and guys," Lil BD said, pulling up to Dirty Perry Street where forty BDs were posted and chilling, but on-point just in case some ops slid through.

"I'ma need y'all because I heard these dudes are serious with that murder game," PG said.

Lil BD looked at him oddly. "You know who did it?"

"Yeah, some niggas called Chi'Raq Gangstas. It was all over the jails. I don't know who they are, but I'ma find out and let you know, bro. You family to me and I'ma always put my life on the line for the guys," PG said before hopping out to chill on the block.

Lil BD banged his steering wheel. Since finding out Boss was the face to the crew, he couldn't follow through without planning carefully because even though they had different fathers they were still brothers by blood. Lil BD had a rep to hold in the streets, if he was to let all this shit slide, he would be looked at differently by everybody. Boss may have been his brother but the rest of them niggas down with him wasn't.

Romell Tukes

Chapter 19

Cicero, Chi-Town

"Uhhmmm." Animal moaned and grabbed tightly onto the dining room table chair, his Fendi jeans were to his ankles as Chloe worked her magical mouth on his dick.

"I love this dick, you taste so good," Chloe said, she looked him in his eyes, while sucking on the tip of his dick.

Animal pushed his hips forward, grabbed her long ponytail, and wrapped it around his hand guiding her head up and down. She sucked his dick while twisting her head as she took him a little deeper into the back of her warm mouth.

"Fuckkk, Chole," Animal gritted as his body started to tighten and she went in a faster pace, feeling his pre-cum fill her mouth.

"Give it to me, Papi," she said, deep-throating his whole cock as her face pressed against his public hair.

Chloe bopped her head on the tip section, as she flicked her tongue around the pee hole, jerking his shift up and down as she spit on it.

"I'm cumminggg!" he shouted, he breathed harder as she forced his cock in the back of her throat, feeling his thick milk which felt like a gusher bust into her mouth.

"Mmmmmm;" Chloe swallowed every drop as she got off her knees with her Versace, silk rope wide open showing her amazing body and phat pussy with a light strip of hair.

"You drained me today, babe?" Animal said, pulling up his pants.

"I know," she replied, covering herself, then walking onto the terrace looking into the morning sky.

Animal and Chloe bought a new 1.7-million-dollar condo in an upper-class neighborhood. The condo had five bedrooms, two walk-in closets, 3 ½ bathrooms, marble floors, two fireplaces, a chef's kitchen with a copper form sink, high-end SS appliances, and a spacious living area with a dining area which opens to a beautiful balcony.

"I'ma be back later, you good? When you flying back out to Colombia?" Animal said hugging her from behind resting his dick on her phat soft ass.

"I'ma go back when I'm ready. When are you going to do what I asked you, baby?" she said turning around looking into his cold eyes that she loved.

Just give me some time, I'ma speak to Boss today about it, babe. I told you I got it."

"I know you." She grabbed his dick as it started to grow in her hand.

She kissed his lips before walking inside to get some sleep. Animal took a deep breath as he looked at the morning clouds parting before pulling out his phone to call Boss.

***

Days Later: Westside, Chi-Town

"Thanks for coming on this move with me." Animal looked toward the buildings across the street that were separated by alleys.

"We don't need to be robbing niggas no more. We up, bro. Who is this nigga, anyway?" Boss said looking out of the tints of the Subaru Legacy, up and down the dark, quiet block in L-Town.

"Here he go right here. I been watching him for a minute," Animal said as a nigga hopped out of a black BMW 8 Series 840i with four duffle bags that looked heavy.

The man had a hoodie on as he made his way into the back alley and went down some stairs leading into the basement.

"Let's slide," Animal said bare-faced.

"No mask?"

"Nigga, we ain't been using them shit," Animal replied as he hopped out with a Tommy Gun and Boss with his Draco in tow.

The man stayed low to the wall once he was in the alley until they saw a lower level with stairs leading into a basement section of the six-floor building.

Both men heard voices behind the door so they knew it was more than one person inside as they gave each other a look and a light nod.

Boom!

Animal kicked the door in to see two Hispanics at a table full of money and drugs, rushing for their weapons on the floor.

Tat! Tat! Tat! Tat! Tat! Tat!

Animal let the Tommy gun rip through both men's upper body and bullets busted the keys open as power filled the air.

Bloc! Bloc! Bloc! Bloc! Bloc!

The other Spanish man shot Animal twice in his chest. Boss fired four shots in his face dropping him on top of the four duffle bags he brought in the basement.

"You good bro?" Boss asked Animal who was on the ground, winded.

"Yeah," Animal said, taking off his Gucci sweater showing a Telfan vest strapped to his body as he took it off.

"Since when you start wearing a vest?"

"Don't worry about that. Grab them empty duffle bags under the table," Animal instructed, seeing all the drugs and money on the table and piles of money on the floor.

"A'ight." Boss rushed to throw everything in the duffle bags while stepping over the Spanish men's dead bodies.

"Get them four filled duffle bags over there," Animal told Boss as he was filling up duffle bags with stacks of money.

Boss saw the other dead body with blood leaking out of his face onto the duffle bags. When he saw the murder victim's face his heart stopped.

"You know who the fuck this is?" Boss looked at Animal who looked like he didn't care.

"Yeah, a nigga you just drilled."

"Nah, dumb muthafucker this is my plug's people. Why would you rob him?" Boss shouted.

" Nigga, I ain't know who he was. I just know he was getting big money. Now come on, we gotta get out of here," Animal said zipping up the last duffle bag.

Both men carried out six bags apiece through the alley, but when they made it to the sidewalk, they saw two niggas with guns looking like they were searching for someone dressed in all yellow.

"That's them," one of the Latin Kings yelled when he saw Boss and Animal with bags. When they heard the gunfire minutes ago they had no clue where it was coming from.

Boc! Boc! Boc!

Boss and Animal weaved the bullets, Boss dropped the duffle bags and fired his Draco, killing one of the men with an instant headshot, as the other gunmen took off running already knowing the effects of the Draco.

Animal ran across the street with Boss behind him. Niggas came out of the next building, shooting at the two men. Animal hopped in the driver's seat, Boss tossed his bags in the back, then started shooting toward the four shooters trying to make their way in the middle of the dark street.

Boss climbed in the car and Animal raced off down the street. The Latin Kings were still in the middle of the street shooting at them.

"Bro, if this shit gets back to King Mike, you better get ready for a war. Outta a million niggas to rob you pick my connect!" Boss yelled

"Stop crying, nigga. At least we came up. It's easy to find a new plug, bro, stop tripping." Animal said thinking his boy was overreacting as always.

"Just take me home, you can keep that shit," Boss rubbed his forehead stressed.

***

Westside, Chi-Town

Ra Ra exited his cousin's house in his Prada outfit feeling like money, he was doing good for himself. He had his own crib and bonds on deck, thanks to Malik.

"That's you, Ra Ra?" a voice said coming up the block.

Ra Ra looked to see that it was his big cousin, he hadn't seen in years.

"Oh, shit, B. Stone. What's up?" Ra Ra looked at his cousin's diamond, encrusted Jaeger LeCoultre Duometre watch worth 275,000 and his white gold rope chain.

"What's good little nigga? When you get home?"

"A couple of weeks ago, I just came to check on your mom and shit. I see you doing big things," Ra Ra said checking out his ice.

"You doing good yourself, bro. What you be fucking with?" B. Stone smiled, glad to see that his little, badass cousin was doing okay for himself.

"I be fucking with my Vice Lord homie, Malik. We be out here doing us," Ra Ra said, he saw his cousin's face turn sour.

"Chi'Raq Gangstas, Malik?"

"Yeah. You know him?"

"I'm trying to kill that, nigga. He killed my right-hand man, all them niggas," B. Stone said.

"Damn, bro, I ain't know."

"Look I need you little cousin bring them to me and—"

"Hold on, bro, I fuck wit, Malik. He's like family to me," Ra Ra said cutting him off.

"*Family?* Nigga, you better open your eyes. I'm family, them niggas don't care about you. They're killers, so they play for keeps. This is Chicago, nigga, the land of the snakes and you can only choose one side."

"I know how this shit go," Ra Ra said, upset that B. Stone was trying to make him pick a side.

"Look how about this, I'ma give you a million dollars if you bring them niggas to me, take your time. Update me daily on them, but act normal, show them you're down for the squad," B. Stone said.

Ra Ra started thinking. "All cash?"

"Yeah, but be smart, because them niggas are on point. Just keep doing what you do, I want this shit to go smooth," B. Stone said smiling.

"A'ight, cuz, I got you. Just have all my money," Ra Ra said walking off. "Get my number from your mom!" Ra Ra yelled as he climbed into his Camaro, feeling like he'd betrayed the only nigga who ever looked out for him.

Chapter 20

Southside, Chi-Town

Janelle had just got home from work at the school, she removed her six-inch heels and kicked them off onto her living room showing her cute purple manicured toes. She collapsed on her new Armani living room furniture, then turned on the TV to watch the news, this was her everyday routine. She got up to go into the kitchen to make herself a glass of wine.

Last night Lil BD came over and spent the night in his room after they went out to eat and to a movie. Everybody thought they were boyfriend and girlfriend which was funny because it was the same way when she would go out with Boss.

After pouring herself a glass of white wine, she heard her doorbell ring, and she sucked her teeth. Janelle opened her door, she was speechless to see the man she was deeply in love with years ago looking more handsome now than he did over twenty years ago.

"Hey, Janelle, you look amazing," Ty said looking at her nice curves in her pencil skirt and flawless skin.

"Hi, Ty, welcome home. Come inside," she said moving over to let him inside, she saw that he had two dozen roses and a box of chocolate.

"This is for you," he said walking in and looking around the luxury apartment. "Nice," Ty complimented, walking into her dining room.

"Thank you." She took the flowers and placed them in a vase.

"It's been a while, Janelle," he said as he followed her into the kitchen in his Balmain outfit and DKNY for men perfume.

"It has. What you been up to since you touched the streets?"

"I'm planning on opening a lounge downtown soon," he said lying.

She gave him a knowing look, certain that he was lying. "Oh, yeah? Good, you're focused on a legit life. I'm proud of you because a lot of black men come home and go backward," she said, pouring herself a glass of wine and him.

"I missed you," he said, causing her to almost spill wine on her counter.

"That's good, I'm sure you missed me and the sixty other bitches you had." She handed him a glass of expensive white wine.

"No woman can ever add up to you," he said looking into her beautiful eyes that he always got his soul lost in.

"I know," she said.

They were now face to face, she gulped her whole glass of wine down as she felt their electrifying energy.

Ty leaned in to kiss her soft, glossy lips, she embraced it back. He put her on the counter, she turned into a wild animal and started ripping off her blouse, as he took off his button-up.

Janelle undid her bra and her big, juicy, firm titties popped out. Ty sucked on them like a baby.

"Uhmmm fuck the foreplay, just fuck me," she said feeling his board muscular shoulders.

Ty slid off her pink thong and lifted her skirt up as she undid his belt buckle to see his massive penis. He slid her body up toward him and slowly entered her tight, pussy which was soaking wet.

"God, damn, Janelle" Ty short stroked her tight love box as she divided her thick legs, so he could deeper, he felt so good.

When she loosened up, she started fucking his dick faster and faster as her breast bounced wildly. Ty grabbed under her big ass and started fucking the life out of her.

"Oh, shittt! Uggghhhh," she groaned as her long, thick dreads swung everywhere.

"I'm about to nut," he moaned deep in her pussy ripping her walls apart.

"What! Oh, hell no," she said pushing him out of her because she wasn't on a pill and she wasn't with no nigga nutting in her, that shit was over twenty years ago.

When Ty was ready to cum, he nutted in his hand. She sat on the counter still horny. "That's it, Ty, you better get me off and do what you used to be good at," she said opening her legs wider showing her perfect intact shaved pussy.

"My pleasure," Ty said as he ate her pussy

"Ahhh—oohhh, yessss!" she yelled as he worked his tongue in and out her delicious sex box.

Lust and pleasure danced all over her face. Janelle caught four orgasms that erupted like a volcano, leaving a pool of her sweet juices on the floor.

"How about we take this in the bedroom?" Ty said, standing naked, watching her get dressed, her body was eye candy.

"Nah, I'm good. I have to go food shopping and I'm sure you have to make arrangements for your club," she said.

He gave her a puzzled look. "When you free again, Janelle?"

"Ty, never that was a one-time thing. Thank you, no strings, and have a good day. We're both grown now and that wave for us, you fucked up twenty years ago," she said now fully dressed.

"I understand, no hard feelings," he said trying to cover his true feelings as she led him out of her house.

***

Downtown, Chi-Town

Animal pulled into the auto shop for an oil change in his Lambo, it was a beautiful day outside and summer was near in some weeks ahead.

"Sir, you can leave the car right here. We will be done with it in less than twenty minutes," a worker said coming out of the shop's garage in a dirty jumpsuit full of oil stains.

"A'ight." Animal climbed out with his new iPhone to call Chloe who'd just arrived in Colombia.

Animal used his phone walking off from his car but when he saw the tan Toyota Aualan pulling into the small driveway with two young niggas staring at him, he tried to play it off as if he was on the phone paying them no mind.

***

"That's him right there, bro. He big ass hell," Hitler said, pulling into the auto shop parking lot, watching Animal who was on the phone.

"Let's get it," Premium said with his Glock 40 in his lap watching Animal closely.

Lil BD, Hitler, and Premium made plans to kill every Chi' Raq Gangsta by any means. Animal was first on the hit list just because he was a BD and killed Loso.

"Let's go," Hitler said as he jumped out like a madman.

Before they let off any rounds, Animal spun around with a 30-round clip on a 50cal.

Bloc! Bloc! Bloc! Bloc! Bloc! Bloc! Bloc! Bloc! Bloc! Bloc!

Animal had the gunmen ducking behind cars as they shot back wildly, missing him, but killing two civilians.

"Don't stop, nigga, kill me!" Animal fired shots toward the Toyota and Range next to it.

Hitler popped off shooting ten rounds as Animal kneeled next to his Lambo and sirens could be heard. Animal got in his Lambo racing out of the other exit. Hitler and Premium got the fuck outta there also before Chicago PD arrived on their bullshit.

Chapter 21

Downtown, Chi-Town

Boss was in his car lot outside his dealership talking to a couple looking at Benz 650.

"This monster has an amaranthine everlasting engine and it's light on gas," Boss said as he checked out the Benz.

"I believe this is it," an older white lady said to her husband.

"We'll take this one, sir," her husband said.

"Okay, you can go inside. My secretary will print all the proper documents," Boss said, as he saw C. Boy's Porsche 911 Targa 4 GTS pull up.

"Will do," the husband said, leading his wife into the dealership. She was excited to receive her Birthday gift from her husband.

Boss made his way to C. Boy who had a badass Spanish bitch in his passenger seat. She was staring at him a little too hard, but he was used to the attention.

"C. Boy, what's the vibe?" Boss asked, embracing him.

"Out here paper chasing. How you doing? I see business is good," C. Boy looked around the lot full of brand-new luxury cars.

"Everything is crisp," Boss said in a Jamaican accent.

"I saw on the news that our situation was handled correctly," C. Boy said referring to seeing Smitty's murder on the news.

"Yeah, one less of a problem. You got your blocks back?"

"Shit we got the whole Westside besides a couple of blocks you and Malik got," C. Boy said.

"Good."

"There is about to be some shit because some niggas just killed King Mike's people over there. Them Latin Kings niggas be putting that pain down," C. Boy said shaking his head.

"I heard. But what's up, you ready for me?"

"Yeah, I'ma need two-hundred keys on the next drop-off, bro. The cash is set, and everything is in place."

"Okay, I got you in a couple of days."

"Cool, just hit my phone." C. Boy walked off.

Boss thought back to King Papi's situation, he was still mad at Animal for putting him in that type of situation. Now he had no choice but to ready it out with his friend no matter the outcome but he hoped nobody saw them that night.

***

C. Boy pulled out of the car dealership thinking about a bag, he was down to his last seventeen keys.

"Is that guy's name, Boss?" the Spanish chick said in the passenger's seat, wearing booty shorts and a tank top showing a lot of skin.

"How do you know that?"

"The night your brother was killed, I heard all of the commotion and the gunshots. I lived next door and the walls were thin. As they were leaving, I saw Face out of my window with two other dudes and I heard one of them call him Boss."

"Bitch you better not be lying."

"I swear that's him, I remember his face, walk, dreads everything. Cash Boy, he killed your brother Sin G," she said.

He had a sinister look in his eyes.

C. Boy was known to most as Cash Boy and he was Sin G's little brother. The guy who was murdered a couple of years ago by some niggas called Chi'Raq Gangstas. Now it all made sense to C. Boy. He knew Melissa wouldn't lie to him he'd been fucking with her since they were kids. The night Sin G was killed she was the first to find his body and call the police.

***

Harold's Chicken Spot:87ᵗʰ Street

"The shit's a different type of chicken, my nigga," Ra Ra said walking out of Harold's Famous Chicken spot, eating a drumstick with Malik behind him.

"Harold's, okay, but Sharks on one-hundred and twenty-seventh Street is litty, bro," Malik said walking down the block to see Lil BD coming his way with another nigga dressed in all black in 92-degree heat.

Boss showed Malik his little brother BD a while back, they met once at a shopping center. Since killing Smitty and taking over his blocks, shit had been amazing. He was eating and so was Ra Ra who changed his Camaro for a red McLaren 600 LT Spider with a rear wing attached to the back.

"You know these niggas?" Ra Ra said, seeing BD and Premium's funny movement.

"I hope so," Malik said, he saw the two men pull out guns from under their shirts, he dropped his chicken and went into action.

Boom! Boom! Boom! Boom!

Boc! Boc! Boc! Boc! Boc! Boc! Boc! Boc!

Bloca! Bloca! Bloca! Bloca!

Gunsmoke filled the street and the gunfire went back and forth for sixty seconds straight.

"Ahhhh shit!" Ra Ra yelled, Lil BD hit him in his leg making him fall on the curb and Malik held him down.

Premium and Lil BD was behind a van twenty feet away from Malik trying to knock his top off but he couldn't get a good shot.

"Aye freeze!" a police officer on a bicycle dressed in shorts yelled out racing around the corner.

Premium shot the cop seven times while Malik and Ra Ra got away.

"Come on, we got to go before the police come. You just killed that nigga," Lil BD said running past the cop's dead body to the Infiniti parked up the block.

***

"Who the fuck was them niggas? Ohhh," Ra Ra said while in pain, he grabbed his shot leg and put his T-shirt and pressure around it to stop it from bleeding.

"That was Boss' little brother. Do you know somebody who can sew you up?" Malik said looking at all the blood Ra Ra was getting on his leather seats in his Maybach.

"Yeah, go to my sister's crib. I'ma kill them niggas that's on the gang," Ra Ra babbled all the way across town, annoying Malik. He had other shit on his mind, like how was he going to tell Boss his little brother just tried to drill him.

***

Southside, Chi-Town

Boss was on his way to his mom's crib to check on her, while on his way in her building, he saw Imam Sa'id coming from the Mosque in his Muslim garment.

As-salaam-alaikum, young brother," Imam Sa'id said smiling as always.

"Wa-alaikum-salaam. How you doing, Imam?"

"I'm blessed. Come upstairs for a second," Imam Sa'id stated, then they both took the elevator upstairs.

Once inside Imam Sa'id's crib, he took off his Louis Vuitton red bottom shoes and inhaled the strong fragrance of Muslim Oil.

"What's been going on?" Boss asked.

"Same thing, I haven't seen you at Jummah in a while. I just wanted to make sure you were okay."

"I just been a little busy."

"I'm very apprehensible and understandable when it comes to worldly matters, but you're a Muslim now just try to focus on your deen."

"I got you, I been slacking," Boss admitted.

"It happens," Imam Sa'id added, he saw Boss looking at a picture of her daughter.

"Who's this?" Boss said looking at a photo of a sexy, thick, light-brown skinned chick standing in front of a huge mansion with palm trees.

"That's my daughter."

"Where she from?"

"You know I'm full-blooded Trinidadian, but she lives in the Port of Spain in Trinidad."

"That's a crazy mansion."

"Yes, she is a very wealthy woman and successful," he added smiling thinking about his daughter who was the same age as Boss.

The two kicked it for an hour then Boss went to spend some time with his mom who took him bowling something he hadn't done in months.

Malik was blowing his phone up, but he figured it could wait because he rarely got time to spend with his mom these days.

Romell Tukes

Chapter 22

Bogota, Colombia

"You did good, Papi. Now all you have to do is stick to the plan and play it cool, then the game will be ours." Chloe hugged up on Animal in her large Jacuzzi connected to her pool in the back of her baroque luscious and rich mansion.

"I know the plan but if Boss catches wind of it, we will both be dead," Animal said, shirtless in the pool as she rubbed her titties on him using her sex appeal to seduce him into doing whatever she pleased.

"Baby, he will never find out. That's why we have to stay two steps ahead of him. You already slipped once by killing the wrong person, babe. We can't afford this to happen again."

"I had no clue King Mike was out of town. I thought King Papi was King Mike. Damn! You can't blame me"

"If King Mike finds out Boss had something to do with King Papi's death, he will kill Boss and most likely someone will kill King Mike. Then boom Chicago's drug trade is ours. You see it's not that hard," she said smiling.

Chloe was using Animal to clean up Chicago streets so she could take over because she saw Chicago as a goldmine. When she met Animal and did her research on him, she knew he would be perfect for her future plans. She wanted to rebuild her empire in the states since she already had Colombia. Training a man like Animal was harder than she thought because he had more muscles than brains and not to mention he was an amateurish hustler.

"It will come together."

"I'm sure it will, Papi. Just take your time, you have an army and drugs on your side. Boss water will run dry real soon. Let's go for a swim, then go for a ride on my Yacht. I want to fuck on white sand while watching the stars," she said as she swam off in her off-white bikini.

"Can't wait," he said chasing after her.

Animal was pussy whipped there was no in between, but he didn't feel right crossing Boss because the two had a real friendship and he never showed him signs of disloyalty. As for Malik, he disliked him a lot. He couldn't wait for the day to put a bullet in his head.

He knew Chloe had big plans for them to take over the drug trade in Chi-Town but to do that he would have to cutthroat and snake a lot of niggas.

***

RJ ended a call with some of his soldiers in Ibague, Colombia who had a big gun battle early this morning with the Santos Family, their rivals. He was in Chloe's office thinking about how to handle this situation because he knew Hector was in Miami, but his capo Mark was the real issue.

RJ got up to look outside in the back to see his sister and Animal swimming and laughing like little kids. He disliked Animal and all black people for that matter, but he knew his sister was up to something, but he couldn't put his finger on it yet. He knew his sister was a King Cobra snake with two heads, she couldn't be trusted at all. He saw that she'd crossed and killed a lot of people to get where she is now.

RJ called his wife to tell her he was on his way home as his guards waited for him outside because the beef with the Santos Family was at an all-time high.

"RJ, I didn't even know you was here," Chloe said coming inside the mansion dripping wet in her bikini with Animal standing behind her with a hard-on, ready to fuck her but now mad that RJ had stopped them.

"Our guys got hit while you were playing love birds," RJ said walking past them ice grilling Animal.

***

Downtown, Chi-Town

Boss was chilling with his pops in his nice, fancy condo chopping it up about everything but mainly sports, they were both big Brooklyn Nets and Atlanta Hawks fans.

"I'm proud of you, kid. You doing good in life, now all you need is a family—some kids because you have a beautiful wife. You better keep her because niggas is thirsty to catch an Instagram model like her," Ty said, laughing.

"Yeah, facts, She wants to open another salon but it's hard for her to maintain one," Boss said sitting on his pops fur loveseat.

"Open another one, it will all come together youngin' the key is to expand. It's just like the dope game," Ty said, pulling out a picture from his wallet.

"I guess you right."

"Here, this is a picture of your sister I recently spoke to her mother, but I still haven't spoken to her yet," Ty admitted.

"Damn, she's beautiful." Boss tried to recall if he'd seen her face somewhere. "Where she from?" He handed Ty back the picture.

"No, keep it I have more but I believe she's from the Southside or Westside somewhere. Her mom isn't trying to give me too much info. She don't want me to approach her or nothing like that until she speaks to her first and I respect that," Ty said, drinking Patron out of the bottle.

"That's fair. You been out of the girl's life forever, so I can see and understand her point of view," Boss said honestly.

"Yeah, you right but ain't no telling how long I'ma be on this earth. My days are getting numbered, son. I've done a lot of things in my life."

"What you mean, Pops? Is everything a'ight?" Boss raised his eyebrows.

"I will never lie to you, son, but I have a lot going on out here. Some niggas trying to kill me," Ty said seriously, taking a sip of Patron.

"Who?"

"It's a long story, kid. I don't even know who these niggas is. My man and childhood friend told me about them before they killed him. Smitty was a good man, they even killed his family. These streets are vicious," Ty said sadly.

Boss swallowed a gulp of spit down his throat when he heard the name Smitty because Boss was the one responsible for his death and family's death.

"Damn."

"Yeah, but, I'm always two steps ahead of the game," Ty said with a laugh as Boss got uneasy.

"Why you say that?"

"Because I dropped a bag on them niggas head. I don't care if it's twenty of them. They all should be dead by the end of the week. Rules to the game, kid, never get your hands dirty instead wash them clean while counting money."

Boss just stared at Ty, his dad, the man who'd just put money on his head.

"You got any names?"

"I don't need you to get involved, son. You're doing good, stay legit," Ty said feeling the Patron give him a little buzz. "The main kid's name is Boss. I got the whole city on his ass."

"Oh, yeah?" Boss said as he pulled out a big Colt .45 handgun pointing it at his dad who looked shocked.

"You need to put that away! What do you want money or drugs? All you have to do is ask," Ty said giving his son the evil eye unable to believe this was happening.

"Nah, pops, I'm Boss the nigga you put a bag on," Boss confessed.

"Ain't no fucking way you, Boss!" Ty said serious, as his eyes grew in fear. He couldn't believe the whole time the enemy was in his front yard.

"Boss at your service, nigga. I started Chi'Raq Gangstas a few years back with the guys and we turned into a big success," Boss said.

"So, you gonna kill your father?"

128

"You was going to kill me so I have no choice. I gotta play for keeps, it's a cold game out here pops. The streets raised me, you couldn't from a jail cell. Maybe if things woulda been different but enough of that," Boss stated.

"I guess I'll be seeing you in hell."

"No question!"

Boom!

Boss shot his pops in the side of his head then ran out of his condo. The police station was across the street so Boss knew the gunfire could be heard at least a block away. Boss ran down the staircase to the back exit and hopped in his car, getting outta sight as tears dropped onto his lap. He never imagined he would have to kill his Pops. A navy-blue Yukon truck was tailing him trying to keep up with Boss as he sped down the streets running red lights and stop signs.

Romell Tukes

Chapter 23

Boss and Rosie were on a private jet to Haiti for a week getaway and to spend some time with each other. Since so much was going on in both of their lives they'd forgotten that they were married.

When Malik told Boss his little brother BD tried to take his head he couldn't believe it, he was confused, he knew it had to be a mistake.

Since Boss was Haitian, he only felt it was right to go back to his roots, this was his first time going to Haiti.

Janelle was born there so she gave him the best areas to visit and the best areas to stay away from because Haiti's poverty neighborhoods were vicious.

"I'm so glad we both took time out to come out here," Rosie said lying in his lap in a Dolce & Gabbana white, mini-dress looking captivating as always.

"It was long overdue, baby," Boss said rubbing her curvaceous ass and sliding his finger under her thongs, entering her tight moist pussy.

"Mmmm, Boss, you better stop," she said, sucking on her breath as her body shivered in ecstasy.

"Or what?" he said, pulling out his dripping wet finger.

She sucked her juices off his finger as if she was sucking his dick. She quickly unbuckled his Hermes belt on his Marc Jacob pants as he stood up.

"Damn, slow down," he said as she took off her dress.

"The plot not coming out right?" she asked, now ass naked showing her toned, curvy body that most men lusted for.

"He's driving the jet," he said as he sat back down with his dick at attention.

He was face to face with her pussy. Boss spread her pussy lips and sucked on her swollen clit, softly as she moaned lifting one leg on the chair's armrest.

"Uhmmmm shit!" she moaned, his tongue game felt magical in her pussy. After she climaxed, Rosie sat on his dick, slowly letting his massive dick open her tight walls.

"Whose pussy is this?" Boss said forcing her waist lower onto his dick and forcing his way inside her.

"Uggghhhh, yours, daddy!" she screamed wrapping her arms around his neck, bouncing up and down on his dick, and kissing his soft lips.

The way her pussy squeezed tightly around his dick made him go crazy, her pussy lips hugged his dick while her juices coated it.

"I'm cumminnggg fuck me harder," she moaned and started throwing her ass in a circular motion as a chute waterfall of cum poured out her love box.

Boss bent her over, lifted one leg on top of the chair, and started to kill her shit from the back causing her to go crazy.

"Bossss, yesss!" she screamed, feeling him knocking at her guts door.

She felt like she was in seventh heaven dancing with Jesus. Minutes later, they both came hard and went to take a shower in the back before the flight was due to land in twenty minutes according to the message on the flatscreen TV.

***

Port-Au-Prince, Haiti

When the jet landed, and they were a couple feet away from touching the ground they were both in love with the tropical trees and humid air.

"It feels so good out here," Rosie said as they walked to the two black Range Rover made for mountain climbing.

The man standing at the driver's door said something in Creole. Boss knows it was in Creole because his mom spoke it on the phone all the time.

Rosie started to speak Spanish and Boss laughed. "Creole, babe, it's broken down French."

"Nigga, I know what Creole is," she said with an attitude before climbing in the truck. The Haitian man did a quick gaze at her beauty. "We're English," Rosie clarified.

"Oh, okay," the man said using his best English accent because that was their 3rd language.

"You know the hotel we're going to?" asked Boss.

"Yes, the best resort on the island," the man said as Boss got in the back looking over his shoulders to see two other Haitian men in the other Range Rover.

"Who are those guys behind us?" Boss asked

"Security for our tourists. We're in the capital of Haiti and a tourist area, so we have to be safe," the man said, driving out of the landing strip area.

As they were riding through Port-Au-Prince they saw a lot of food stands, fruit stands, beautiful Haitian women, and men. They saw shopping areas, tall buildings, boat docks, restaurants, clubs, and a chain of hotels with every race of mankind walking around.

"This is our tourist spot. It's beautiful as you see. The best clubs and restaurants lay here on these blocks," the driver said as he made a left down toward a private gated beach community.

When they got to the hotel resort on a private beach, they were amazed as they pulled into the front of the glass and cobble stone-built majestic.

"Wow, this looks better in person," Rosie said walking inside to see servants waiting for them with trays of fruit and wine.

They walked around the marble slab floors as a beautiful Haitian woman led them to their suite in the rear back near the majestic oceanfront gulet, pavilion, olive trees, and the outdoor lounge space.

Once in the suite, they were amazed to see large mahogany glass doors, volcano ash bathtubs, soapstone countertops, open floor plans that allowed sunlight to filter throughout the suit, spacious en-suite, a secondary bedroom, and fancy paintings.

Boss gave the servant a tip and got himself comfortable while Rosie had jet lag and went to take a nap in the huge bed with the rails and curtains covering the bed.

After two hours of just sitting around, Boss came up with the idea to go pick up some food so he could cook for his wife. He left his gun in the bedroom before he made his way to the lobby area.

"I'm trying to go shopping," Boss told the Haitian man who'd picked him up earlier from the airport.

"It's a little dark out, we don't normally go through the shopping district this late," he said, the other two Haitian looked at Boss as if he was crazy.

"I'ma be fast."

"Okay, come on," the man said as another Haitian man stood with him to leave. They took one truck and drove through the city with Boss in the back.

The inner city looked different at night. He saw homeless people, thugs, weapons, hookers, drug dealers, and people rushing to get home or to their destination.

"Why it look so crazy out here at night?" Boss asked.

Both men laughed.

"We have a lot of dangerous powerful people out here that make the Zoe Pound look like church-going people," the driver said as he stopped at a red light.

Bloc! Bloc! Bloc! Bloc! Bloc! Bloc! Bloc! Bloc!

Bullets ripped through the Range Rover, Boss ducked and the Haitian men were dead. Six men wearing masks hopped out of the van parked on the side of him and snatched him out yelling in Creole. When Boss was inside the big van the men bridled him to the floor punching him in his face and body until he stopped restraining and fighting.

Five minutes later, the van pulled into a rocky trail which led to a large barn area. The men tied Boss up as if he was an animal about to be slaughtered. They dragged him into the barn area which looked like a torturing chamber. Boss was laid in the middle of the floor surrounded by sixty Haitian men with assault rifles and swords. One of them took Boss' wallet and keys smiling as he did with a swift motion of his finger cutting his throat. It didn't take Boss long to figure what was going down.

"Fuck you," Boss spat, he saw a tall, dread head nigga come out the back.

The crowd made an opening for the man dressed in a suit and tie.

"You come to my city on a private jet and stay at the best resort. Why would you set yourself up like that?" the tall Haitian man said in good English.

"I'm just here to enjoy myself."

"Well, you picked the wrong place to do so."

"I see," Boss said.

A Haitian passed the tall Haitian men who had to be the leader. The man looked through Boss's wallet to see his ID and a couple of family photos. The tall Haitian man looked at Boss for two minutes without blinking before he rushed off to the back and got on his phone.

Boss saw a couple of goons whispering to each other until the tall Haitian came back out. He was yelling in Creole and the six goons who grabbed Boss came forward in a line. Boss then saw something he couldn't imagine. The leader took one of their guns and shot all of them in the head, then faced Boss, untied him, and gave him his wallet.

"I'm very sorry for this mistake, please forgive me," the man said respectfully, Boss nodded. "My people will take you to your hotel. You will have no problems as long as you're on this island," he told Boss before yelling something in Creole to his goons and they led Boss out.

As Boss was leaving, he looked back to see the man staring at him awkwardly. When he got in the van, they drove him back to the resort.

When he walked into the lobby, he saw eight Haitians pacing back and forth, they saw him and looked shocked.

"They let him live; this is a first," one of them said.

"What was that about?" Boss asked

"You're lucky, that's why we don't travel at night through the shopping district. The people who got a hold of you run Haiti, they are dangerous they never let nobody go. Who are you?" one of them asked as Boss walked off shaking his head with a busted lip.

Inside the suite, he saw Rosie walking around with puffy eyes in a robe smoking a cigarette.

"Oh, Lord, babe!" she shouted, then jumped in his arms with her ass hanging out. "They said you were dead! What happened?" She felt his busted lip.

"Nothing, love, everything is good. It was a misunderstanding."

"You want to leave first thing in the morning?"

"No, we're going to stay and enjoy ourselves. I'ma go take a shower." He kissed her forehead.

Rosie was a nervous wreck when she heard about him being killed in an ambush. Seeing him made her realize how much she really loves him. She dropped her robe and went toward the shower to show him just how much.

Chapter 24

Westside, Chi-Town

Malik arrived in the church parking lot for Sunday service dressed to impress in a Tom Ford suit. He wasn't at church to get saved, at least not today. He was on a mission. After getting into a shootout with Lil BD, Malik wanted to know who the other nigga was with him.

It just so happened that Ra Ra recognized the gunman's face. Premium a nigga he'd done time within the county jail a few years back. The only thing Ra Ra knew was that Premium was a BD gang member and his parents were deacons at a church on the Westside.

Malik took the information from Ra Ra and did his own research, which led him here today with a picture of an older, brown-skinned, tall woman with a birthmark on her face.

There were tons of people walking into the church in high spirits ready to praise their Lord.

"Morning, young man, may the Lord bless you." An old lady greeted him at the front door as she did everybody.

"You too, Ms," Malik said walking through the double doors to see and hear people screaming, shouting, and dancing up and down the aisle. He thought he was in a club, he coulda sworn he saw a lady crip walking as he took a seat in the far back.

It didn't take long for him to spot Premium. She was on stage sitting down clapping her hands to the church music and tapping her feet.

Malik played along waving a Holy Bible bopping his head to the beat as he saw two church cuties wink at him and he smiled back. He was still grieving over what happened to Simone. The two females were a distraction at the moment.

He saw Premium's mom get up and walked through the dancing toward him, he got nervous. She gave him a smile and nod as she made her way through the church double doors.

Seconds later, Malik got up and followed her. He saw her walking down the hall and made a right into a restroom area. Malik looked behind him, he saw the coast was clear and he smoothly slid into the women's bathroom. The noise of farting and someone shitting disturbed his thought process, he covered his mouth to the strong powerful aroma of shit. Malik saw feet under stall two, he pulled his gun out and kicked the door open. Premium's mom screamed falling off the toilet exposing her bushy, nasty pussy.

Boc! Boc! Boc! Boc! Boc!

The shells dropped on the floor as the bullets pierced her heart and lungs killing her within seconds. Malik left the church with no remorse, he felt an archetype evil spirit enter his soul.

***

Westside, Chi-Town

Ra Ra waited for B. Stone outside a Walgreens shopping market early in the morning, looking around nervously hoping nobody would spot him.

His big cousin waited for an update on the status of his progress in bringing him close to the Chi`Raq Gangstas. An all-white GMC truck with tints pulled into the Walgreens parking lot blowing its horn.

Ra Ra made his way to the truck and hopped inside, looking around to make sure he wasn't being followed.

"What happened to meeting up only at night?" Ra Ra asked in an angry manner.

"Shit changed. What's been going on?" B. Stone asked.

"We had a shootout a while back but this nigga went to the nigga's mom's church to kill her yesterday. These niggas is audacious, bro. I think we should fall back," Ra Ra said, B. Stone just stared at him as if he'd lost his mind.

"Where's the other two?"

"One is out of the country and I barely see the big, evil-looking nigga," Ra Ra explained.

"Okay, try to get more shit so we can make our move," B. Stone stated.

"We—hold on, my job is to bring them to you, and I get paid. I've seen these niggas gun game. It's like they're trained killers."

"Nigga, I don't care about none of that."

"A'ight I got you," Ra Ra said, hopping out of the truck, walking to his Honda Accord.

***

Lil BD was parked across the street watching Ra Ra hop out of the truck with the license plates that spelled B. Stone. Lil BD knew who both men were because he'd been doing his research on Chi`Raq Gangstas and their rivals. This scene didn't make any sense to him at all. There was only one reason for Ra Ra and B. Stone to get together and that was a double-cross.

Lil BD now knew the Chi`Raq Gangstas had a lot more to worry about than him and his crew.

***

Days Later

Ty's funeral was packed with Black P Stones from all over the city and state because he was an active high-ranking member of the gang.

Janelle sat in the front, dressed in all-black with shades over her eyes, and Boss on her sat on her side listening to the ceremony given by Imam Sa'id who'd known Ty Stone since he was a kid.

Boss saw a lot of familiar and unfamiliar faces as he just sat there with a vibe showing no type of emotion. He lost no sleep after killing his father because he knew it was him or his pops and one thing he'd learned from the streets was to play for keeps.

When the speeches were over, Boss helped five other men carry his pops casket as they prepared to bury him.

"Boss, I'm sorry for the loss. Your father was a good man. He didn't deserve to die in vain, but take care of yourself," Imam Sa'id walked off, then stopped. "In life, we always have to conceal a third eye for many reasons that we shouldn't but that's just how it is," Imam Sa'id stated before walking off to where eight big Muslim niggas awaited him at a limo.

"You ready?" Janelle said snapping him out of his thought process as she caught wind of it. "You good, baby?"

"Yeah, mom I'm straight."

"Good, come on, I'ma cook dinner. I told your little, narrow ass brother to come down to show respect," she said climbing in her Range Rover and Boss rode with her.

"It's good he may have been busy."

"That's not the point and you know it. But how was Haiti?" She smiled, glad he'd finally made a visit to his roots.

"It was nice, a little dangerous down there. But it's a beautiful country."

"Yes, it is, I visit twice a year and I stay at the same resort you did," she said driving behind a long line of cars exiting the graveyard.

"How you know I stayed at a resort?"

"You told me when you called me."

"Oh, I musta forgot," he replied

"Your father was a good man, but he had a lot of bad karma," she said

"Don't we all."

"Guess so. But next time you plan to kill a family member. Close his eyes, let him die in honor," she said before turning on the radio.

Boss thought he'd just heard wrong. There was no way she knew he killed him and his mind raced with questions.

Chapter 25

Downtown, Chi-Town

Rosie was at her hair salon in the restroom pissing on a pregnancy stick to see if her gut feeling wasn't deceiving her. Lately, since she came back from Haiti, she'd been vomiting and having serious stomach pains throughout the day. She thought she was having a stomach virus from some shit she ate in Haiti because they were eating all types of exotic shit.

She saw the stick had two lines which indicated she was pregnant.

"Yesssss!" she screamed, smiling, then she pulled out her phone and called Boss to tell him the good news.

Rosie's dream was finally coming together all she ever wanted was a family and a happy life. She realized he wasn't picking up because he was at the car dealership so she went into her office and grabbed her purse, so she could meet him home with a surprise candlelight dinner to tell him the good news.

"Erica, lock up tonight I have to go home," she told one of her workers as she made her exit out the salon.

"Okay, mami, ride that thing good tonight. I see the look in your eyes," Erica said laughing, a couple of other women laughed along just so Erica wouldn't fuck their hairdo up because she was vicious like that.

***

"Good to see you, bro," Boss said, taking a seat in his office with King Mike who'd just arrived. He was fresh in town from his trip.

"Likewise, bro, but I'm coming back to the loss of my right-hand man. Some niggas killed, King Papi," King Mike said emotionally.

"I'm sorry to hear that, man. I re-upped from him once and I never heard from him again. I hope you find the nigga who did this shit."

"I will sooner than later because my guys had a shootout with the killers. He saw their faces and remembered one of them but he didn't want to tell me over the phone. I'ma speak to him as soon as I settle in," King Mike said with a murderous look in his eyes that Boss had seen too often nowadays.

"If I can be any help let me know I got you, big bro."

"Gratitude, but I just want to let you know the shipment will be tonight at our same location. Niggas robbed me for kid change, Boss. That wasn't even a stash house they robbed," he said, laughing.

Boss shook his head thinking about how dumb and thirsty Animal was. "Damn, but I'll be there tonight."

"A'ight take care," King Mike said standing up. "Boss you're very few people I deal with that I can vouch for, that has never crossed me or had to worry about. Bro, I respect you for that," King Mike said sternly before he walked out.

Boss took a deep breath because shit was about to hit the fan and he didn't have a plan.

He saw two new texts on his iPhone screen both from Rosie asking him to come home asap and the other said she loved him very dearly.

Boss grabbed his shit and left, he already had a headache, he felt as if his life was going downhill, thanks to someone else's downfall.

***

Days Later

Premium was having his mom's wake in a small house owned by the church Pastor, churchgoers were mourning and crying all over the place.

"I'm with you, bro," Hitler said sitting next to Premium in the living room, cries could be heard throughout the house.

Since Premium lost his mom, he'd been an emotional wreck, he was really fucked up about it because he knew it was his fault she was in a casket.

"Good look, Joe, but I don't need you to commiserate or feel pity for me. I'ma soldier, I'ma go get some air," Premium said standing to leave.

All the older women evil-eyed him because they had a feeling it was because of her son's street life.

Premium wore gang flags to his mom's wake with a pistol poking out of his skinny jeans. Hitler followed him outside to see him smoking a blunt of weed. The Pastor came outside in a gray suit.

"Son, can you not smoke outside my home? I know you're going through a lot of issues, but the Lord will—"

"Nigga, shut the fuck up!" Premium said as shots went off.

Tat! Tat! Tat! Tat! Tat! Boom! Boom! Boom! Boom!

Malik and Ra Ra aired the front of the house out as Hitler and Premium took cover shooting back. The Draco bullets made them run inside over the Pastor's dead body. Malik and Ra Ra ran off leaving six women left dead and the pastor. Hitler and Premium made it out without a scratch on them.

Romell Tukes

Chapter 26

Downtown, Chi-Town

King Mike called Boss to come down to the boat dock on the Chicago River Side so he could speak to him in private. It has been days since King Mike came to his office to see him about what happened to King Papi.

Boss pulled into the parking lot as the sky darkness covered the river. He saw King Mike parked alone in Bentley Coupe with fishbowl tints.

Walking over to King Mike he felt his stare as he tried to shake it off and put on his poker face. Boss knew if King Mike thought he was responsible for King Papi's death, he woulda been dead.

King Mike was Rosie's brother so it wouldn't be too hard to find him, he spent many nights at their home.

"Boss, what's going? I see you dripped out in Givenchy," King Mike said, checking out his outfit.

"You know how we do. What's good?"

"I found out who hit my spot. A kid name Animal. I believe he's a BD from Buff City. One of my guys used to fuck his sister before she got hit up," King Mike said

"That's crazy I've never heard of him, but I can get my people on it," Boss said, trying to look straight.

"Gratitude but my people are already on it as we speak. One of my homies who got away said he saw a nigga who looked like you—" King Mike said with a pause as Boss's heart started racing.

"Me?"

"Yeah, but I told him that had to be a mistake. Because love and loyalty wouldn't do that, right?" King Mike said as he turned his head like an owl to look him in his eyes like he was taught to tell if a nigga was lying or not.

"Facts, I would never even think of some shit like that."

"Good, but he said it was dark out anyway. So, it coulda been anybody," King Mike said as he started reaching under his seat.

Boss ain't give him a chance to get off on him, he pulled out his Glock 40 and shot King Mike in the head four times.

Boss went under Mike's seat and pulled out a duffle bag full of money. King Mike realized when Boss people paid for the bricks, he sent him days ago, he gave him $82,500 extra so he just wanted to give him what he owed him.

Boss felt dumb but he knew eventually he would connect Animal to him, so it was better to get him out the way now. He left Mike's corpse slumped in the Bentley seats as he hopped out with the duffle bag in hand.

The only person he could think about now was Rosie. He pulled off because she had a close relationship with her brother. To make shit worse she was now pregnant and last night she said how she planned to tell King Mike the good news at his birthday party on his Yacht in two days.

***

Southside, Chi-Town

Malik was at a gas station in the hood pumping gas feeling the summer heat as he felt his waves and forehead sweating bullets.

Ra Ra was waiting for him across town because they had to meet with Boss. Malik had been hearing in the streets that C. Boy wanted Boss dead. Malik asked around about C. Boy's resume and street ties, come to find out his real street name was Cash Boy and he is Sin G's brother a Kingpin nigga they robbed years ago.

It wasn't hard to figure out that C. Boy musta got wind that Boss was with the Chi'Raq Gangstas but they had to get rid of him quickly. Malik and the gang had too much beef and ops to be worried about a no-name nigga. So, he was on his way to holler at Boss.

The beef with Lil BD and his crew was taking a toll on him because Boss told him to handle his business but just don't kill Lil BD. Malik wasn't going to let no nigga take his life if he can prevent it.

A silver Volkswagen CL Sedan with tinted windows halfway down pulled into the station. Malik paid it no mind as he got done pumping gas.

Bloc! Bloc! Bloc! Bloc! Bloc! Bloc! Bloc! Bloc! Shots shattered his glass windows, he shot back at the Volkswagen, as the driver sped out of the situation.

Malik saw the car was long gone, he jumped in his Audi S8 Sedan sky blue pulling off wondering who just tried to take his head off.

***

Downtown, Chi-Town

Malik was parked in the back of Boss' dealership recreating the scene that had just happened minutes ago at the gas station. He called Ra Ra to pick him up but for some reason, his phone kept going to voicemail.

"That shit happened so fast on the gang, bro. I'ma have to get me a vest out here. We got so many ops, I don't know who is who," Malik said, Boss laughed always one for making a bad situation into humor.

"I had to take care of King Mike. He was on to me from that shit I told you that me and Animal did."

"We need a new plug now?" Malik asked.

"Yeah, but we got enough work to hold us over until we find one."

"Good. That kid C. Boy, his real name is Cash Boy, he was Sin G's brother."

"Sin G?" Boss said not remembering the name because he'd done so much dirt in his lifetime it was all hard to keep up with.

"Nigga, our first big lick or second. The Spanish nigga."

"Ohhh, yeah," Boss said as it came to him.

"He wants you dead, but I got a plan. I know some people in his circle. His guys fuck with my guys and nobody likes him," Malik stated.

"Cool, I'ma get back to work and check on Rosie, she's sick about her brother and she's pregnant to make it worse."

"I know you was telling me. Congratulations, I'm the Godfather, right?"

"You wouldn't let me live if you wasn't."

"Cool. Have you seen Animal around lately? I hope he not ducking no rec out here," Malik said.

"I have no clue, Joe, I just let him do him. That nigga fried."

"True," Malik said, climbing in his car to leave.

***

Westside

"What the fuck we doing here, nigga?" Ra Ra said as Malik park in the nursing home parking lot on bingo night.

"I'm just visiting an old friend. What's good with your leg?"

"It's better. Although, I still feel sharp pains in that bitch sometimes," Ra Ra said texting a chick on his phone, she was telling him to come to the strip club so they could spend some time together.

"Shit getting crazy out here somebody tried to take my top off earlier. I ain't know niggas still do drivebys," Malik said with a light chuckle while watching the building closely.

"Shit a nigga will kill a nigga any type of way nowadays on foot, on bikes, walk-ups, roofs."

"Facts, bro," Malik agreed.

"We still going to the club tonight?"

"Yeah."

"A'ight let me Facetime this bitch," Ra Ra said as he Facetimed a stripper bitch he was falling for.

"I'll be right back." Malik hopped out in a rush as he saw an older woman and an old man with her laughing.

"I think they just finished Bingo night, young man," the older black man said to Malik as he saw him coming their way.

"Thank you!"

Boc!

Malik shot him in the face, then shot B. Stone's mom in the head four times.

Once he was back in the Audi, Ra Ra was looking around to see what had happened. Malik pulled off as if nothing had gone down.

"You good?" Ra Ra asked.

"Yeah! You ready to hit the club? It's only nine-thirty p.m. but I'm sure Sky11 is litty," Malik said.

Ra Ra shrugged his shoulders not caring where they went.

Romell Tukes

Chapter 27

Southside, Chi-Town

Boss was planning to spend time with his mom today, he had plans to take her out to dinner like she used to do him every Friday when he was a kid. Boss climbed out of his Rolls Royce Dawn Coupe feeling like a true boss. He saw a brand-new, fire red Maserati with tints and it was clean. He wondered who it belonged to as he walked into his mom's building. He saw his little brother walking out in a pair of Saint Laurent shorts and shirt to match with a Jesus piece diamond chain swinging.

"You gonna double-cross your own blood?" Boss said as they stood six feet away from each other in a vicious stare down.

"*Double cross?* Nigga, you and your crew been crossing up the city. What, you thought it wasn't going to catch up with you?" Lil BD stated.

"Nigga, I ain't cross you."

"Yeah, but you killed my big homie," Lil BD said.

"Big homie? Nigga, what he ever do for you? We don't respect no big homie shit, especially a rat," Boss said getting Lil BD upset.

"I ain't see no black and white, so I ain't about to stamp that," Lil BD said lying because he'd seen eight statements with Loso's name on it, he even took the stand on a nigga ten years ago. "I ain't got time for the small talk. You know what's up," Lil BD said walking past Boss.

"So, you an op now?" Boss asked seriously as he stepped.

"When you see an op drill an op. Karma is a bitch and you got more to worry about than me," Lil BD said laughing as he walked down the stairs of his mom's building, feeling the nice warm summer day breeze.

Boss didn't know what his little brother meant by his comment, but he never thought he would see this day when he would have to go against his own brother. Growing up they were very close, they couldn't stay away from each other for more than a couple of hours.

Seeing no other choice left, he knew if it came to it he would have to kill BD, but he knew he would never be able to look his mom in her beautiful face.

**

Later That Night

Boss was in a supermarket that was open 24/7 looking for beef jerky, canned peaches, and yogurt for Rosie who texted him those items to get because she was craving those foods. After he collected everything, he made his way to the cashier who'd been standing on her feet for over twelve hours.

"Nice hairdo," Boss said to the cute, red-bone chick who looked like she shoulda been a model instead of a cashier in some supermarket.

"Thank you, I did it myself," she said smiling and looking him up and down at him, admiring his Rag & Bone jeans and Christian Dior top as well as his big face GMT Master Rolex watch filled with diamonds.

"You like this job?" Boss said as she got done ringing up his items.

"Does mice like cats?"

"Guess not."

"I'm just waiting to finish hair school, so I can find a real job doing what I like," she said.

Boss saw how perfect the home girl's body was. "Look, take this card, go here in the morning, and ask for Rosie. Tell her I sent you." Boss handed her Rosie's Salon business card.

"The Rosie Salon I been here before, it's downtown. That shit is lit," she boasted.

"Yeah, that's my wife's shop. Tell her I sent you."

"Your wife?" she replied awkwardly.

"You good, I'ma tell her now. She's good people," Boss stated.

"Thank you," she said as Boss walked out.

Boss saw a young man with a hoodie covering half of his face walking toward him and his Rolls Royce. It was so dark out Boss couldn't really tell who the dude was.

"You thought you was low, nigga?" the kid with the hoodie asked, raising a gun.

"You got the wrong nigga, bro," Boss said as the gunmen pulled his hoodie off.

"Ra Ra, it's like that, bro? That's how you do the squad?" Boss asked.

"Nigga, shut up. You don't know shit. Y'all niggas think y'all can just go around killing people? This nigga Malik just killed my cousin in front of me. I'ma get all of you fuck niggas," Ra Ra said with tears in his red eyes because he'd been drinking, and Boss smelled the liquor on his breath.

Boss saw a silver Volkswagen CL Sedan creeping with the headlights off and the windows halfway down as he continued to listen to Ra Ra babble about his life story.

Tat! Tat! Tat! Tat! Tat! Tat! Tat!

Bullets exploded through Ra Ra's head and blood squirted all over Boss's face. Boss hopped in his Rolls Royce racing out of the lot, the Volkswagen was already gone. Boss had no clue who that was or who'd just saved his life, but he was thankful.

As Boss drove down the expressway doing the speed limit so he wouldn't get pulled over, he thought back to when he spoke to Malik and he said a silver Volkswagen with tints tried to kill him at a gas station. Boss' mind went into overdrive, he wondered if those bullets were for Ra Ra or him.

***

Chicago Heights

Malik was leaving his crib on his way to check on Boss because he'd told him about what happened last night with Ra Ra. Not in a million years did he think Ra Ra would try to back door him and his crew after everything he'd done for him. He had no clue Ra Ra was related to B. Stone, if he did, he woulda been killed him. Malik stopped at a stop sign to see a red Maserati Coupe with tints pulled up on his driver's side. Malik was about to make a right until traffic continued to hold him at the stop sign.

He looked out of his window to see the Maserati's window roll down and Lil BD was smiling while pointing a Tech-9 at him.

Tat! Tat! Tat! Tat! Tat! Tat! Tat!

Malik hit the gas smashing into a Ford F-150 pick truck. The Audi swerved past the truck with the bumper hanging off and his back window and side window broken.

"Bitch ass nigga!" Malik shouted while driving down a main street.

***

One Week Later: Robins, IL

C. Boy aka Cash Boy was in his old hood in Robins, IL getting money while forming a plan to get at Boss and his crew. He had the manpower, he just needed to focus on how he was going to bait him in. C. Boy was in a hole in the wall strip club alone, watching a couple of dancers twerk on the small stage, as he drank out of the Henny bottle. C. Boy loved women more than money, his brother Sin G used to always tell him he had his priorities fucked up.

There was a cute, thick, light brown-skinned chick on stage who looked like she was black and Korean. C. Boy felt his dick getting hard as he watched her slide backward on a chair making each ass cheek pop one at a time.

After her song and stage time was up, she went to the back dressing room to get dressed to leave as she did every night.

C. Boy was so gone mentally off her, he was thinking about going back there to get her for a private show. When he saw her come back upstairs in a sexy red dress with heels, he followed her outside.

"Excuse me, beautiful!" C. Boy shouted as she stopped in the club parking lot to turn around hoping it wasn't another stalker nigga.

She saw his Dolce & Gabbana outfit, icy chain, and watch then thought she could stop to hear the handsome, Spanish man out.

"Yes?"

"I'm Cash Boy, and I'm not stalking you or nothing. I saw you on stage and you're beautiful. I would love to wake up to your face every morning."

"Let's start with, I'm Cinnamon," she said with her thick, juicy lips as she stared at him with her Chinky eyes that drove men crazy.

"I'm just trying to spend some time with you."

"Time is money," she said smiling.

"That's my language," he said, pulling out a big wad of blue faces.

"Where is your car?"

"The Denial truck over there," he replied.

They made their way to his truck. Once inside she had his dick in her mouth, deep throating him and going crazy as she put her two tongue rings to work.

"Shitttt," he moaned as she bobbed her head up and down in a slow, then fast motion. He couldn't hold on no more and nutted in her mouth, she slurped it all up and spit it out on his dick.

"You got a condom so you can fuck me? Hold on I got one," she said reaching into her bag, he was in love.

Boom! Boom! Boom!

Cinnamon shot him in his chest, then exited his car and headed to her Benz. She called her Vice Lord homie Malik who paid her to drill him. She was a Vice Lord and a stripper. She was for the guys.

Romell Tukes

Chapter 28

Southside, Chi-Town

The past couple of weeks Animal had been staying out the way and away from drama, so he could focus on his game plan. Now was the perfect time to take over the city's drug trade with Smitty, King Mike, and Boss without a plug everybody was out of the picture. Chloe's plan worked perfectly, he was surprised at how smart she was. Having her supply of coke assured that he was on his way to the top, so he focused on building his own empire with the help of two recruits.

Animal used the name Black while he operated his business. He had a strong destituteness and thirst for power and illustriousness.

"That's them right there," Day-Day said as a Benz truck with HD lights pulled into the high school parking lot.

Day-Day was Animal's face to his drug trade, he took care of all business transactions while he played the background.

"Make sure you tell them one-hundred or better and anything over five hundred keys we drop the price four points," Animal said looking at his BD homie who'd just come home from jail broke and fucked up.

He met Day-Day a couple of weeks ago in a Footlocker. After they chopped it up for a while Animal was feeling his vibe and he knew the kid needed some help to get on his feet, so it all worked out perfect.

"I got you, Black." Day-Day hopped out of the Lexus LX black on black.

Ten minutes later, Day-Day hopped back in the car smiling.

"They said they want six hundred because the three hundred they copped last week moved in days. They said their shit is pure. They're moving the work in Iowa. You know it's a goldmine out there," Day-Day said smiling.

"Good, let's go get it ready," Animal said, pulling out of the school's parking area on his way to the stash house.

***

Meanwhile

Boss had to stay a little late at work tonight with Kylie. They had to do inventory on the new car shipment.

"Kylie, it's almost eleven p.m. I gotta go. You staying?" Boss asked the cute, red-head he'd seen come a long way in life from a crackhead hooker to a classy boss bitch.

"Go home, I got this. I don't have shit else to do, so I'll see you tomorrow," Kylie said, sitting at her desk going through a lot of paperwork.

"Get home safe," he said exhausted from the long day.

He walked outside to his Rolls Royce parked near the front entrance. Boss had been focused on work, family, and trying to find a new plug because he was running low on work. He had no more than 725 keys left and his VA people put in an order for half of that amount.

Malik got rid of Cash Boy recently so that was one less problem but his biggest problem was his own brother. He knew Lil BD was hard-headed and stubborn at times just like him but going to war over a snitch nigga was goofy to him. Malik wanted to take his brother's head off his shoulders. Boss held him back just until Lil BD came back to his senses. Boss saw someone pop out from between two cars.

Bloc!

The shooter hit Boss in his leg making him fall. Boss grabbed his gun, but the gunman kicked it out of his hand making it fly under a Range Rover.

The gunman wore all black with a hoodie and ski mask but Boss was able to see the eyes. Boss know who the shooter was as they made eye contact. Boss saw the gunman's hand trembling as if the shooter didn't want to do it or was confused.

Bloc!

The shooter shot Boss in his shoulder before running off.

"Ahhhhhh!" Boss yelled in pain as Kylie came running outside in her heels with a bat in her hand ready to put in work.

Boss saw a silver Volkswagen with tints race away as he bled uncontrollably.

"Should I call the police?" Kylie tried to help him up.

"No, take me to the hospital," Boss said and she led him to her Benz.

***

At the hospital Boss' wounds were more serious than what he thought, so he had to stay a couple of days to undergo surgery for his leg or they would have to cut it off if they didn't fix the damaged tissue and broken ligaments.

The police came to ask Boss what happened. He told them he was leaving work then he blacked out in the parking lot after feeling pain but he didn't remember what happened. The Chicago PD was just happy they didn't have to do no paperwork because they had over 47 murders a day sometimes, so they were busy with real shit.

Boss told Kylie to call his mom because she called his phone twice in the recent hour as she did every night to check on him.

Kylie wanted to stay the night, but he had to force her to leave so she could open up the car dealership in the morning.

He was lying in the hospital bed when he saw his mom walking past his window in a sweatsuit with her dreads in a ponytail.

"Baby, you're okay?" Janelle rushed to his aid, seeing his leg in a cask and his arms hooked up to IVs.

"Yeah, I'm straight. Thanks for coming."

"Of course, they tried to tell me visiting hours were over. I went crazy on them crackers. But anyway, who did this? What happened?"

"Mom, I don't want to talk about that."

"You know who did it, don't you?" she replied.

"Did you call Rosie? I hope not I'll be out of here in days."

Romell Tukes

Chapter 29

Bogota, Colombia

Chloe was in her personal office on her laptop, wiring some money to Miami to the Peru Cartel Family who supplied her with the purest form of dope in North American. The only organization that had better dope than the Peru Family was the Mexican Cartel in Mexico City.

"Chloe, you busy?" RJ asked walking into her office in slacks and a button-up.

"Not at all, RJ," she said sliding back leaning in her recliner chair, as she placed her Jimmy Choo heels on her desk crossing her legs. Whenever she wore a mini dress, she failed to wear any underclothes.

"We still going to open the Cabaret tonight?" RJ asked she gave him a confused look. "The club."

"Oh, you should've said club. I was thinking we should reschedule it because I have to fly back out to Chicago," she said.

He stared at her with a funny look. "What are you up to?"

"Don't worry about that. Did you go check on mommy?" she asked.

"Yes, but answer my question. Because I know you have something up your sleeve. I want to know because I know you're not in love with that big dummy. He's your disguise and pawn to something else, something big."

"Animal is a big help to my plans and I'm a big help to his. So, fair exchange is never a robbery. Chicago is a goldmine, and we can make a lot of money," she said standing up, pulling her tight mini dress down that stopped inches away from her pussy.

"I already know that part, but there is something or someone bigger you have in mind. As your brother and business partner, I think you should let me in on it," RJ said as Chloe stood in front of him and sat on her desk.

"You may debilitate my plans. I don't think your position within my organization qualifies to know certain things," she said, opening her legs wider, showing her phat pretty pussy.

RJ took a quick peep at his sister's perfect shape pussy then focused back on her eyes and she smiled at him.

"I just thought we was a team," he said in Spanish, his dick was about to explode in his pants.

"You thought wrong, but maybe if you get with the program, we can become a team," she said lifting one leg resting it on his leg as she exposed her whole pussy.

Chloe then did the unthinkable and started playing in her pussy, making wet noises as she moaned loudly. RJ was numb and his dick was rock hard. He knew this was wrong but his sister was one of the baddest bitches he'd ever seen.

"Uhmmm I'm cumminggg," she said making her fingers pop faster and faster in and out her pussy. When she came thick white creamy cum poured out slowly.

She took two fingers swapping her juices on her fingers, she placed her fingers in his mouth and he licked the cream off her fingers. Chloe then got on her knees and rubbed his hard dick through his slack, then she pulled it out.

"Chloe," he cried out, her hand had the magic touch.

"Shhhhhh," she said, seeing pre-cum pouring out of the tip.

Chloe deep throated his whole dick up and down four times. He let off a big load in her mouth within seconds as she ate his dick up. When his dick went limp, she laughed wiping his cum off her chin as she swallowed her nephew/niece.

RJ pulled up his pants and rushed out of her office. His legs felt like noodles soaked in water too long. He would never admit it, but Chloe's head game was the best, he'd never came that fast and he was embarrassed.

Chloe watched him leave the mansion, she laughed. Ever since they were kids, she remembered she used to be in the shower, and he would jerk off to her from outside the bathroom door. He would always stare at her body and lust over her. So, she knew it would be easy to seduce him and a little blowjob could never hurt. Chloe got back on her laptop to email someone, thinking about how good RJ's dick tasted.

***

Downtown, Chi-Town

Rosie was on her way to the hospital this morning to pay Boss a visit. She knew something was wrong when he didn't come home last night and especially when his phone went to voicemail every time she called him. She called Janelle and she explained that he was okay, he just was at the wrong place wrong at the wrong time. Rosie called the hospital, and they told her visiting hours were from 7:00 a.m. to 9:00 p.m. on weekdays. She was in her Lexus truck drinking her morning coffee, looking at the small bulge in her stomach that always brought a smile to her face.

It's been three months since she found out she was pregnant. She felt as if life couldn't be better. After losing her brother King Mike she started to feel hopeless until she realized the baby in her was replacing him.

Rosie pulled into the hospital parking lot looking for a parking spot because the lot was just about full. Rosie found a spot at the deep end near the back. She did her make-up in her car mirror since she couldn't do it at home because she was in a rush. She saw some black dude come to her window, so she rolled her window down.

"Good morning," Rosie said respectfully.

"Good morning. Do you know where I can find the ICU entrance?" he asked.

Rosie looked at the hospital trying to remember because she been here many times. Before she could reply the man pointed a gun at her, she screamed.

"This is for your husband," B. Stone said.

He heard a nurse yell, "Stop! He had just gone on his smoke break.

B. Stone fired two shots into the truck before running off like a bat out of the darkness.

The nurse saw the whole thing, even when both cars pulled into the lot. B. Stone was following Rosie since yesterday when she left her hair Salon. B. Stone was waiting for Boss to come home all night but that never happened. Since Malik killed his mom outside of the nursing home on Bingo night, he'd been laying low. Since Ra Ra was killed, he had no inside help, so he had to watch and stalk.

The nurse saw Rosie was still alive and breathing as he grabbed her out of the truck and carried her through the hospital emergency doors.

"Helppp!" the nurse said rushing her into the back as doctors and nurses help to aid him to save her life.

After two hours of working on her, they sent her to the ICU unit to watch over her. Luckily, they were able to get the bullets out but unfortunately, she'd lost the baby. The pills she was given had her knocked out and unaware that the love of her life was next door.

Chapter 30

Southside, Chi-Town

Mrs. Brown lived in a small house on 107 Champion Street a Four Corner Hustler hood where she raised her grandson Hitler. Mrs. Brown was seventy-eight-years old and she received home Health Aid seven days a week through her medical insurance. Normally a different health aid nurse would come to her home from 8:00 a.m.-4:00 p.m. to help her clean, get around the house because she used a walker, cook her meals, and make sure she took her meds. She also needed help washing her ass and changing her diapers.

Hitler came by at least twice a day to check on her, but he was so caught up in the street life, it was normally a hi and bye.

"I'm on my way one second!" Mrs. Brown yelled in her old raspy voice she'd gained from years of smoking. It took her close to five minutes to get from her living room couch to her front door.

"Come in," she said when she saw the light-skinned man in a nurse's uniform with scrubs.

"Mrs. Brown, I'm here to help aid you today," the man said as he walked inside with a small bag.

"I know they send a new person to my house every day like this is the crack house. That will be next door. I'm glad they sent a handsome young man," she said using her walker to snail walk back into her living room. "I would like to take a bath today. I have a little itch I need scratched if you know what I mean," she said sitting down on her old lady dusty couch.

Mrs. Brown was a freak, she was still beautiful for an old woman, but she ran off a lot of male workers because she was doing a lot of things that were not appropriate. One worker fell asleep and when he woke up, he saw Mrs. Brown with her teeth out sucking his dick. She played in her pussy in front of another worker while he was cooking her lunch.

"Let's start with your meds," the man said as he pulled out a taser and heavy chains.

"Do you have plans for those? Because I'm not as flexible as I used to be and my pussy is a little wide but if you're packing, we should be good," she said.

The man looked at her as if she was crazy. Malik wasted no time as the taser hit her neck putting her down. Malik started swinging the chains across her face until he busted her face wide open. Blood was all over the couch and living room floor. Malik then pulled a hammer out of his bag, climbed on top of her corpse, and slammed the hammer into her face constantly until he saw her flesh hanging out her head.

"Damn," Malik said. He packed up his shit and left the bloody house before the real health home aid nurse arrived.

Before Ra Ra was killed, he gave him some info about Hitler and his grandmama's location so Malik stored it in the back of his brain. That was one thing he liked about Ra Ra he knew all the young gangstas around the city. When he tried to kill Boss and crossed his guys that shit crushed him because he was a solid little nigga.

Malik was headed home to take a shower then he made plans to go pay Simone's gravesite a visit. There wasn't a day that went past that he didn't think about her or his love he shared with her. He felt as if her death was his fault. He hadn't had a peaceful night's sleep since her death, but he knew death was part of the game. He only wished B. Stone woulda took him instead of Simone.

***

Days Later

Boss was out with Animal in a Tom Ford store doing some shopping. He was released from the hospital two days ago and Rosie should be released in less than 24 hours.

When he found out by Malik who'd come to visit him that Rosie was next door in critical condition he was sick. When he was able to see her, she was awake but as soon as she saw him, tears filled her eyes.

The news of them losing their child broke him and her, but they were grateful to have each other still after almost dying.

Boss asked her if she remembered who did it and when she described the gunman, Boss already knew who it was, B. Stone.

"How's wifey, bro? I can't believe B. Stone almost did a number on her," Animal said as if Rosie was a street nigga in the field drilling shit.

"*Did a number on her!* Bro, she's a civilian," Boss said with a dysphoria attitude.

"True, but you have to remember, my nigga. This is Chicago ain't no such thing as a civilian or an innocent bystander, bro. Look at all the civilians we killed," Animal said.

Boss tried on a Blazer in a mirror. He couldn't even say shit because he knew Animal was a hundred percent correct, no one was safe especially in a time of war.

"This shit's a good fit. I be wearing suits all day at work. So, I'm getting adjusted to a more classy attire. Balmain jeans are cool, but that shit is getting played out," Boss said looking at Animal's Balmain tight-fit jeans and T-shirt with a Balmain logo covering his chest area.

"Nigga, who do you think you work for John Gotti or Al Capone?" Animal said laughing.

"Nah, I'm just a bossed-up nigga."

"Nigga, you look a limousine driver," Animal said.

Boss grabbed a couple of outfits he was leaving with. "Regular hating nigga, but I been meaning to speak to you," Boss said as he gave all his outfits and belts to the cashier.

"What's up?" Animal asked.

"The streets been talking."

"About what?" Animal stroked by in a defensive tone.

Boss caught his demeanor. "Damn, bro, calm down. You good?"

"Yeah, I was just asking," Animal said as they walked out of the store.

"Word on the street is that someone is moving a lot of weight out here. We need to find out who because the city was in a big drought before this new nigga popped up, but I think he's from outta town," Boss said walking through the mall.

"You need a plug, don't you?"

"Hell yeah, that's why I need to reach out to whoever this nigga is," Boss replied.

"Smart, you don't know his name or where he be at? It's nice to get a nigga's attention. Today all we gotta do is lay some shit down."

"Nah, that's not called for, money and violence don't mix," Boss said, making it to the lower garage level in the mall.

"What you want to do?"

"I'll figure it out," Boss said as they hopped in his Rolls Royce on his way back to the hospital to look over his face.

***

One Week Later

Today was the hottest day of the summer and Hitler was in a front-row seat at his grandmama's funeral surrounded by family and friends. When he'd received the news of his grandmama's death it hit him hard because she'd raised him since a baby. Hitler didn't know who personally killed her, but he knew who was responsible for her death. The Chi'Raq Gangstas had their name all over it. His grandmother's face was so damaged and decomposed that they had to have a close casket ceremony.

After everybody paid their respects, Hitler, Lil BD, Premium, and Jenny stayed back to comfort him and show their support.

"Don't stress, bro, we're going get them niggas lacking," Premium said knowing how it felt to lose a close family member because he'd lost his mom and dad to the Chi'Raq Gangstas.

"I know," Hitler said staring at his grandmama's photo, trying to hold back his tears.

Lil BD was about to say something until he looked across the field at the two graveyard workers digging holes while peaking at them. "Something ain't right about—"

Tat! Tat! Tat! Tat! Tat! Tat! Tat! Tat! Tat! Tat! Tat! Tat! Tat! Tat! Tat! Tat!

Shot from two street sweeper assault rifles made everybody hit the floor.

Lil BD pulled out his Glock 45 with 30 extra rounds and fired back and Hitler did the same.

Boom! Boom! Boom! Boom! Boom! Boom! Boom!

Lil BD covered Jenny who was on the floor praying that Lil BD ain't get hit as he went bullet for bullet.

"Premium!" Hitler yelled, finally seeing him on the floor with two big holes in his neck as blood poured out. "Shit yoooo, Lil BD, we gotta go!" Hitler screamed as the two gunmen, posted up behind trees trying to dodge Lil BD's wild shot.

Lil BD grabbed Jenny and ran to their car as Hitler followed waving bullets from Malik and Animal. They pulled off in a Yukon truck and Malik and Animal were still chasing them down with powerful assault rifle 223 bullets.

Romell Tukes

Chapter 31

Miami, South Beach

Chloe walked on the beach's hot sand enjoying the beautiful summer day in her Celine bikini with her ass hanging out showing off her curvy body. As she walked past crowds of people stared at her sexually. She finally found who she'd come here to see.

"Chloe, you look beautiful, please join me," Victor said as he stood up from his tent and folded chair. He had four big guards surrounding him as always, which Chloe never understood because if a person wanted someone really dead, then it would be done especially in the Cartels.

"You still look twenty and handsome," Chloe said looking at his tanned skin, short hair, tone & lean built, and nice perfect set of teeth.

"I'm pushing forty-nine next week with no grays. I'm trying, but how are you doing?"

"I'm good just opening some new lanes in the states trying to expand," she said, getting comfortable in the folding chair as the small umbrella tent blocked the sun from burning her flawless skin.

"You're opening shop in the states? Wow, I know a lot of blood is about to be spilled." Victor already knew how dangerous and deadly she was.

"No blood spilling, just mind-controlling."

"Wait, please don't tell me you plan on opening shop down here, Chloe? Because you know the Santos Cartel will rage war against us both," Victor warned.

"No, Victor, I'm not. I'm in Chicago but I do plan on buying a new house out here," she explained.

"Chicago, why out there?"

"It's a goldmine, Victor. The blacks are seventy-five percent of the city and the drug trade is nothing like I've seen before," Chloe honestly informed.

"You trust the niggers?"

"No, but I trust business and they're good for business."

"Good for you, but what do I owe this visit to? Because I know you didn't come to Miami to look sexy, now did you?"

"Well, I need a Heroin connect and you're the best dope plug I know."

"Thank you how generous to say, but I'll pass, Chloe. Every time another Cartel does business with you it doesn't take long for you to cross them or kill them," Victor stated truthfully, shaking his head.

"Victor, I never crossed a soul unless he planned to snake me. We always had a good connection, I need you. I will bring you millions."

"It's not always about the money because all money ain't good money," he said calmly.

Victor was the head boss of the Peru Cartel Family, he controlled 65% of the dope street named *Dog Food* that came into America through Miami ports.

"You will have my loyalty. My word is all I have," she said watching kids and people enjoy themselves in the water.

"Give me some time to think this out, Chloe. You have a lot of enemies. With business your issues become my problems," he said.

"I know how to handle my enemies. It's my friends I have to worry about," she said getting up to leave, the string was swallowing her ass cheeks as it jiggled and lightly bounced.

***

Southside, Chi-Town

"How you been? I see you heal up quick just like when you was a kid. I swear you used to go outside come back in with ten new bruises on you, then after a warm bath and a good night's sleep you'd be healed," Janelle said as she brought food out from the kitchen and placed it on the dining room table.

She'd cooked a big meal today: fish, greens, mac & cheese, chicken, curry rice, jerk beef stew, and all types of Haitian desserts.

"I guess it's the Haitian in me, but why you cook so much if it's just me, Rosie, and you?" Boss asked as Rosie came out from the back using the restroom.

Rosie wore a red slit dress with heels, her amazing elegance always sparked the room. "That smells so good," Rosie said as she reentered the room and sat down next to her husband.

Suddenly the doorbell rang.

"Hold on," Janelle said as she went to answer the door.

Seconds later, Lil BD walked into his mom's house smiling in a Dior outfit with sunglasses to match his black and white fit. When Lil BD saw Boss sitting at the dinner table, his face quickly turned into hatred.

"Sit down, boy. What's wrong with you?" Janelle said sensing the bad energy and vibes from both her sons.

"I'm good, mom, I gotta go," Lil BD said as he turned to leave.

Boss had a serious face ready to end his brother's career if he was to move wrong. Boss pushed the button to have Malik and Animal shoot up Hitler at his grandmama's funeral.

"What the hell is wrong with you, kids? Y'all brothers, same blood. Y'all going to need each other one day," Janelle told both of them before she heard her front food slam close. "I know his little ass ain't just slam my damn door?" Janelle took a deep breath as she sat down.

"Can I say a prayer?" Rosie asked, easing the tension.

"Sure," Janelle said.

She always liked Rosie she was perfect for Boss. Rosie prayed and they all ate a big Haitian meal laughing and telling stories.

***

Olympia Field, IL:Next Day

Rosie was in Angela's living room admiring the beautiful 18,117 sq ft mansion, high 45ft ceilings, and the Versace wall to wall carpet.

Angela was her dead brother's wife, her and King Mike had been a couple since they were kids. They had a real strong relationship, so his death took a toll on her the worst. She even thought about suicide many times since his loss, but she had his three kids to raise. She was a thirty-two-year-old, beautiful, Spanish woman, petite, colorful eyes, big breasts, long curly brown hair, and a perfect heart-shaped ass.

"I'm glad you're okay. I was so scared when I came to visit you," Angela said in her soft, sweet voice as she sat on her Versace couch Indian style.

"I was scared, I'm from the hood. I'ma Latin Queen for life, but I've never been shot and that shit burns," Rosie said drinking a glass of wine with her like they used to always do before King Mike died.

"Did you ever find out who did it or what for?"

"No, but I believe someone thought I was the wrong person," she replied lying.

Rosie knew it was someone who wanted revenge because B. Stone said Boss' name, so she wasn't dumb. She knew he was still in the streets.

"That happens a lot gurl, but they still have no leads on my husband's murder. The police said it was a premeditated murder," Angela said.

"Chicago PD never knows shit," Rosie complained.

"I know the last person he said he was going to see was your husband," Angela added as she took a gulp of her red wine.

"Huh—Boss?" Rosie questioned with a puzzled look because Boss told her he hadn't seen her brother in months which was weird to her if he was still getting drugs from him. She also remembered that her brother went out to Puerto Rico for a while.

"Yeah, Boss!" Angela confirmed. "Look I want to show you something." Angela got up and went behind the bar to get some papers and her purse. "Look at this Rosie, this is Mike's call log. His recent conversations were all with Boss." Angela handed her the papers.

Rosie read the papers and it was Boss' number texting Mike saying, *//: I'm on my way.*

Another text read, *//: I'm here.*

"What are you trying to say?" Rosie said now looking up to see Angela standing over her with a gun pointed at her, and tears flowing from her face.

"Your husband killed my soul, bitch! Stand up *now!*" Angela shouted.

Rosie did as she was told while staring at the 9mm Beretta. "We can talk about this, Angela. I'm sure we don't know one-hundred percent if this is true, let me find out first."

"Bitch, are you that dumb? Boss is a fucking Chi'Raq Gangsta, the streets talk about him. I tried to warn Mike, but he said Boss would never cross the line, and now look," Angela cried as tears fogged her vision.

Rosie saw her chance to make a move as Angela wiped her eyes. Rosie rushed her and tackled her to the floor, the gun slid underneath the couch. Angela pushed Rosie off her as she tried to get the gun. Rosie punched her in her face twice, slowing her down as she went for the gun. Angela grabbed her ankle, Rosie kicked her in her nose, it started bleeding.

"Ahhhhh!" Angela yelled as Rosie was able to get the gun.

"You stupid, bitch," Rosie said with an evil look in her eyes. She trained the gun on her.

"Kill me, bitch, I have nothing to live for," Angela cried.

Rosie fired the gun six times into Angela's upper chest, her body went into shock before her eyes and rolled back in her head, then she coughed up her own blood.

Rosie ran quickly out of her house with her purse outside to her new Range Rover and drove off. Halfway down the street, Rosie pulled over to vomit on someone's lawn. She'd never killed anybody so the gruesome scene made her stomach flip.

Romell Tukes

Chapter 32

New York City

"It's so many people out here, baby," Jenny told Lil BD as she held his hand walking through the busy Time Squares area.

"This was a good idea." Lil BD crossed the street shoulder to shoulder with civilians.

Looking at the sky raised buildings Lil BD felt it was past time for a small getaway and Jenny felt the same. She'd just landed a new job in a Chicago hospital. It was Jenny's idea to come to New York and sightsee, go out to some clubs, restaurants, and shopping. New York was known for its extravagance shopping areas downtown and hottest clubs especially gentlemen clubs.

"Can I ask you something? Would you like to spend the rest of your life with me?" Lil BD asked seriously as he stopped in the middle of a four-way street.

"What are you doing? Come on, boy, before this light turns red," she said as the cab driver blew the horn at them. She looked beautiful today in a Chanel summer sundress with six-inch heels and her hair in a bun.

"Would you?"

"You know I want to spend the rest of my life with you. Now let's go," she said.

He got on one knee and everybody cheered and yelled. Lil BD pull out a box and showed her the GIA certified diamond ring 159 at D color WS2 clarity worth 300,000

"Oh, my fucking God! BD—"

"Will you marry me?"

"Yesss!" she yelled crying as the cars all blew their horns yelling and cheering for them as well as the crowds of people.

The two wanted to get married in New York and luckily a city hall was blocks away from the Time Square section. They spent a whole week in New York before they went back home to Chi'Raq as a married couple.

***

Downtown, Chi-Town

Boss arrived at work at his car dealership. Today was July 4th one of the busiest days of the year. It was 6:00 a.m. he had a lot of preparing to do. Life at home had been weird for him since Rosie lost the baby. She barely talked to him or even looked at him. All she did was go to work and come home then go to sleep. When he asked her what was wrong, she looked at him and turned on him without saying a word. Her silence was killing him and to make matters worse he had blue balls. Every time he looked at Rosie's curvy body and beauty it would drive him crazy.

Boss opened the dealership turning on the lights getting ready for the big day. Today all cars were 25% off the retail price, so it was going to be a long day. Boss had two Dracos in his office and two AK-47s stashed in the lot because too many things went down at the lot.

***

B. Stone was parked across the street watching Boss' every move like a hawk thinking how dumb Boss was for trying to run a business when he was in a time of war. Today was the day he planned to send Boss to his maker, this been the day he'd been eager for since Boss kidnapped Face.

B. Stone grabbed his MP assault rifle from off his passenger seat and pulled his ski mask over his face because he knew there were cameras inside. As soon as B. Stone opened the door to his GMC truck, he was surprised by an AR-15

"Thought you had one?" Malik said before firing 13 shots into B. Stone's face.

Malik ran down the block and hopped in an old Mazda bussing a U-turn on the empty street making his way back to the Southside.

Boss knew B. Stone was tailing him for the past week, so he had Malik tail B. Stone and play him close. Boss knew B. Stone would see him as an easy target at his place of work especially early in the morning, so he fell into their trap.

***

Later That Night

Boss, Malik, and Animal all met up at their old stomping grounds at Lincoln Park close to midnight.

"That was a smooth hit, Malik. One less problem we have to deal with," Boss said

"You was on point, bro. As soon as I pulled up on his truck this nigga was sliding out with a big ass AR or some shit," Malik said seriously.

"Damn, on the gang? Joe wasn't playing," Animal said sitting on top of a top near the park cook-out area for the public.

"Now all we gotta worry about is my little brother and his crew. But we need to find who this nigga is moving weight through the city."

"What about the nigga who shot you, bro?" Animal asked with concern.

"Since when you start worrying about one of the guys being hit?" Malik laughed.

"Nigga, you talk too much," Animal said.

"The nigga who hit me can wait. Our main goal right now is to find out who out here moving all this weight. When I find a new plug, we're gonna have to reclaim our city. So, I want to know who we will be up against. I do have a name," Boss said

"Who?" Animal demanded with a strong base in his voice.

Malik felt something off about his energy as if he was up to something.

"A nigga name Black, I believe he's from out of town because nobody knows this nigga," Boss stated.

"Just say the word, I can't wait to use this lemon squeeze," Animal replied smiling.

"I'm sure, but I gotta go, don't forget to watch out for Lil BD. But don't kill him, let me take care of him," Boss said before leaving.

"Why you looking at me like that?" Animal asked, watching Malik give him a funny stare.

"A'int shit, bro, see you later," Malik said leaving the park with a head full of thoughts.

***

Chicago Heights

Boss pulled into his driveway to see Rosie's car gone. She didn't tell him she was going anywhere but nowadays she didn't tell him shit. Things were so bad she slept in another room. Boss did everything he could to make peace and figure out what was wrong.

He was not cheating on her, so he was confused as to why she wouldn't want to share the same bed as her husband. Boss know Puerto Rican women were very faithful to men that treated them good but they were also crazy.

Once in the house, he went into the living room to see a long note sitting on the living room table. Boss thought he was seeing shit as he picked up the letter and started reading it.

Dear Husband,

I will always love you and hold you dear to my heart, but when we took an oath in Vegas to love each other I meant it, did you? No, because if you did, you wouldn't have crossed me or hurt me by killing my brother. Yes, I know you did it because I almost lost my life. I had to kill Angela because if I didn't, she would've killed me. So, thank you. I haven't slept since. I can't look at you or even be around you knowing you killed my brother. That shit hurts a lot because I thought I could trust you. Our love was amazing, you're a great man, but I can't be with you after what you did. You can have the house, salon, money, fame, and the game. I was never that type of woman. All I ever wanted was love. I'm leaving for good. I

wish you well in life. Sorry if you're hurting, right now. But you feel how I feel. I'm focused on a new life alone. I have a lot of healing to do. I'll send you the divorce papers. Take care!
P.S I believe this is best for us both. XOXO

Boss dropped the letter on the floor as tears fell with it. He couldn't believe his wife had just walked out on him. He always thought about her finding out, but he'd planned to deny it because he knew she would never see his reasoning to save his own life. He tried to call her, only to hear that her phone had been disconnected. This was the first time in his life that he honestly didn't know what to do.

Romell Tukes

Chapter 33

Downtown, Chi-Town

Chloe and Animal were both tired and sweaty from the hour of rough passionate sex they just had.

"You going to murder my little pussy with that enormous dick, Papi," Chloe said laying on her satin sheets in her fancy condo.

"Well, your pussy is already heaven for me," Animal said kissing her soft lips that she'd just used to suck the skin off his cock.

"How's business? Do the fiends like the dope?" she asked, getting dressed as the sun was rising.

"Business is good, they love the dog food and I'm almost out," Animal said proudly.

He had no clue where she got the grade 10 Heroin from but it was pure. Animal knew she supplied coke, but he had no clue she could get her hands on pure Heroin.

"Good, I'm on my way to Miami later. Did you wire the money like I asked?" She jumped up and down to squeeze her ass over in her Fendi jeans. "I also have another shipment arriving."

"Everything is taken care of, but Western Union blocked me. So, next time I'll use someone else or Cash App," Animal said looking at her round ass sitting perfect in her jeans.

Victor from the Peru Cartel made the decision to give Chloe a shot and supply her with the purest Heroin in Miami. He gave her one warning letting her know she had one time to cross him and he promised to have her head on a plate.

"How are things with your friend? I bet they don't know a thing, I told you a new name will work perfect," she said putting on her heels.

"They on to me; not so much Boss. But I can see it in Malik's eyes. He knows something."

"What? DeWayne this could fuck up everything you've worked so hard to build. You have to do something fast like now, baby. What if he comes for you," Chloe said sitting between his legs on the edge of the bed.

Animal was in deep thought because he knew she was right Malik was a vicious type nigga.

"Do what."

"Kill Malik," Chloe said nonchalantly as she got up and walked to the bathroom to fix her hair.

Killing Malik was never in his plans but Chloe made a point, he refused to let one bad apple spoil his plans to take over the city.

***

Janelle was leaving work at the school after staying an extra hour to grade some tests and prepare for tomorrow's assignments for her students.

It was a nice, cool, summer day not too hot but a little sticky outside. Janelle placed her work bag in the backseat of her Range Rover. She'd just received a text from Lil BD apologizing for the way he acted a couple of weeks ago at her house. He told her to meet him and Jenny at Chow Town, a classy upscale restaurant downtown. Janelle hopped in her Range on her way out of the empty school lot. When she got to an intersection, she saw a black Hummer H2 and van speeding her way.

"Someone in a rush," Janelle said as the truck and van swerved her way instead of going straight. Janelle put the car in neutral and hit the gas pedal, but it was pointless.

The Hummer slammed into the Range almost flipping Janelle over, she was unconscious and comatose as the 7 masked men lured her body out of the damaged Range into a van. The van and Hummer swerved off in the opposite direction leaving the smashed up Range on the side of the road.

***

Southside, Chi-Town

Animal and Malik exited the packed bar after having drinks for Malik's birthday. It was 1:00 a.m. and Malik was drunk, but Animal was sober.

"Glad we can cut here that bar was litty," Malik said with a slur as they walked through the bar's parking lot.

"That shit ain't about shit, bro."

"I can't make it back."

"I got you," Animal said as Malik threw up on the hood of somebody's Ferrari.

"I had too much Remy." Malik bent over, still vomiting.

Animal stood there getting very impatient. "You good, bro. We should get going." Animal patted him on his back.

"Let's go, you a cool dude, Animal. I'm not going to lie, I never liked you. I used to think you was fake," Malik said.

"Damn."

"Yeah, and I thought you was this Black nigga the bro was talking about."

"What?" Animal's alarms went off in his head.

"I was tripping, I can't see you double-crossing the guys like that. We all basically family," Malik said as he approached his Lexus coupe.

"Who else you told that crazy shit to?"

"I told Boss about it, but he said I was tripping and overthinking shit," Malik said.

Animal nodded his head and pulled out a Desert Eagle pointing it at Malik's face as Malik looked at him with double vision.

"You about to kill me, nigga?" Malik said with a laugh. "I knew I was right about you bitch nigga, you a snake."

"True and I play for keeps. I'm Black, you was right but it's a little too late. You should always go with your gut feeling," Animal said with a smirk unaware that someone was watching the whole scene.

***

"Damn, bro, I ain't see that shit coming. This some Juice shit like how Paa did Bishop. You remember that shit?" Hitler asked Lil BD who was in the driver's seat of the Dodge Challenger SRT watching Animal about to finish Malik.

Lil BD had followed them here. He'd been tailing Malik for a couple of hours after he went out to eat with Jenny. His mom was supposed to show up for dinner, but he figured she was still mad at him that's why she turned her phone off but tomorrow he planned to go to her house. He wanted to tell her the news about his marriage with Jenny that's why he asked her to come out with him.

"Let's make our move before civilians come out," Lil' BD said.

"Hold on, let's watch him kill Malik first."

"Nigga, fuck that we about to take both of them niggas out and Boss is for me," Lil' BD said as he grabbed his Draco with 100 shots before getting out with Hitler behind him

***

"I'll see you in another world, Animal."

"Nigga, you talk too much. I been waiting to die five minutes ago," Malik said.

Animal slapped him across the face with a gun, almost knocking him out.

Tat! Tat! Tat! Tat! Boc! Boc! Boc! Boc! Boc!

Animal ducked as he returned fire, Malik ran off to the other side of his car and pulled out his 44 Bulldog.

Boom! Boom! Boom!

The 44 barked loudly as Malik tried to take Animal head off.

Hitler saw Malik trying to kill Animal who was now hiding behind a pickup truck. Hitler shot seven rounds at Malik hitting him in his shoulder.

"Ahhhhh shit, muthafucka!" Malik yelled as he fell to the ground.

Bloc! Bloc! Bloc! Bloc! Bloc! Bloc!

Animal sent rounds toward Lil BD almost taking off half of his face.

"Let's play!" Animal fired more shots until his gun clicked. *Tat! Tat! Tat! Tat! Tat! Tat!*

The Draco bullets from Lil BD put holes through the pickup truck Animal was hiding behind.

Malik climbed in his Lexus and drove off, leaving Animal for dead as police sirens were close.

Lil BD and Hitler couldn't risk going to jail so they jumped into the Challenger, speeding off just in time as a police cruiser entered the other side of the parking where Animal was.

Animal had another clip in the back of his Louis Vuitton jeans, he reloaded his clip.

"Drop the gun!" the officer yelled when he saw Animal point it at him.

Animal fired six shots, hitting the cop twice in his vest before running off through the dark parking lot.

Romell Tukes

Chapter 34

Buff City

Jenny and Lil BD were at Jenny's mom's house eating and having a good time. Jenny's mom was a cool down to earth woman who looked half her age. She was mixed with black, Indian, and Dominican she was a bombshell beauty.

Lil BD now understood where Jenny got her beauty from because her mom was eye candy, if he wasn't married to Jenny then she would be number one on his hit list.

"I'm so happy y'all got married. Y'all look so happy. Young love is amazing, especially with all these young people out here dying in these streets," Jenny's mom stated sitting at the table in her dining room, looking at them both.

"I plan to grow old with him, mom," Jenny said blushing.

Lil BD rubbed his foot on hers, knowing he was trying to be nasty she gave him a look.

"I only wish your father was alive to see this if you would've given him a chance," Jenny's mom said, shaking her head.

"Mom!" Jenny shouted.

Lil BD looked confused because he had no clue her dad was dead because she never talked about him.

"You ain't tell him about your father, did you?" Jenny's mom asked looking at her daughter who had her head down.

"No, because it wasn't serious," she replied.

"He came to your college graduation and gave you three-hundred dollars and you tossed it. Shit, I would've taken that shit. You've lost your mind," Jenny's mom said.

Jenny got up from the table and stormed outside into the backyard.

"She'll be okay, she should've told you like I told her hard headed ass."

"I'ma go speak to her," Lil BD said walking through the kitchen texting his mom to see if she was okay.

Lil BD was supposed to go check on her last night, but he was busy. Tonight, he was going to her house, if it was the last thing he did because she wasn't answering her phone or her texts.

"Jenny," Lil BD called as he saw tears in her beautiful eyes.

"What?" She wiped her eyes.

"Talk to me. How come you ain't tell me about your father? You're my wife now, Jenny. You have to be open and trustworthy to me. I will forever have your back through thick and thin, baby," Lil BD said standing face to face with her.

"My father and I met once. He told me he wanted to be in my life and be a father after all these years that he missed," she said.

"You shoulda gave him a chance."

"I should have, and I was planning to after sleeping on it and he told me I had a brother. I didn't give two fucks about that I just wanted a relationship with him. When he was killed my soul and hopes were ripped away from me again. You know how it feels to see all the little girls come to school with their fathers and everybody looking at you crazy and laughing," she said.

"Yeah, I do. My father is a fiend somewhere, I don't even know how he looks." Lil BD shot back.

"The night he was killed he must have pocket dialed my number by a mistake. I heard a little of the conversation and the person who killed him," she said pausing taking a deep breath.

"Who?"

"Boss!" Jenny cried.

Lil BD's face looked puzzled. "Are you sure that's weird," Lil BD said.

She pulled out her phone and went to the recorded data she'd saved from that night her dad was killed.

Lil BD listened closely, he heard Boss' voice clearly, but he couldn't make out what Jenny's dad was saying except when he called out Boss' name before he heard gunfire.

"Damn, don't worry, baby. I'ma get this nigga." Lil BD was pissed Boss had killed his wife's pops.

"I've been doing me," she said.

"You what?"

"Come let me show you," Jenny said walking into the back alley where her car was parked.

"What's this?" Lil BD asked.

Jenny opened her car door and grabbed some photos of Boss, Malik, and Animal all around town.

"You're a private investigator now?" he said laughing but she was very serious. "Whose car is this?" Lil BD asked looking at the silver Volkswagen sedan with tints.

"It's my car I use when I do my drills and stalking," Jenny said. "You remember when Boss got shot?" she asked.

"Yeah, how you know about that?"

"I did it, babe. I know you got beef with him and he killed my dad, so—"

She was cut off by Lil BD. "You shot my brother? Have you lost your damn mind, Jenny? That nigga will kill you!"

"Fuck all of that! I'm not scared," she replied bravely.

"We gotta get out of town because if he saw you or even has a clue you shot him, your life is at risk."

"I'm not going nowhere until I finish the job," she replied.

"No, you're leaving tonight, we both are until I figure this shit out. Stay here until I get back. I don't know why he would kill your dad. What was your dad's name anyway?" he asked.

"Ty," she said with an attitude because she didn't want to leave but she had no choice.

"Hold on—Ty?"

"Yeah, Ty."

"Ty Stone who just came home from prison?"

"Yeah. How do you know that?" Jenny looked at him as if he had something to do with her dad's death.

"Jenny are you sure?"

"Yes, BD, Ty Stone. Why? What do you know?"

"Ty Stone is Boss' father," he said.

Jenny's heart dropped to her stomach. "Boss is your brother too? So, that makes us—" Jenny felt like she was about to vomi,t thinking BD was her brother.

"No, we not brother and sister. Me and Boss have different fathers, so me and you are not related," Lil BD said.

She looked relieved but still overwhelmed. "So, what now?" she added.

"Stay here, I'ma go to the crib and pack up our shit. We're going to New York for a while but I gotta go check on my mom. I love you." Lil BD kissed her, then he ran through the alley to get to the front of the house where his BMW i8 was parked.

Jenny was shocked none of this made any sense to her. If Boss was her brother, why would he kill their father? The night she shot him in his car lot, the look in his eyes was as if he knew who she was. It was like looking at herself in the mirror. That's why she didn't give him a headshot.

***

Lil BD was on his way to his mom's house since it was closer. He couldn't believe Boss and Jenny were related. This threw a monkey ranch in his plan because if he was to kill Boss, then he would be killing his mom's son, his brother, and his wife's brother. Everything was too much to take in and the city's murder rate was at a high. Niggas was getting slumped left and right all around the city.

He pulled into the front of his mom's crib to see her lights off and her Range Rover gone which was odd because Janelle was always home at night. It was 10:35 p.m. his mom went to sleep at 11:00 p.m. every night it was her routine. Lil BD reached into his glove compartment to get his gun just in case some funny shit was to pop off inside because he had a gut feeling something was wrong.

Psst!

"What the fuck?" Lil BD said as he felt a pain shoot into his neck like a bullet, but it wasn't a bullet.

Lil BD tried to lift his gun but whatever he was just shot with had him in slow motion and dizzy. The driver's door opened and two big strong men grabbed Lil BD and his gun, then tossed him in the black Ford Explorer XLT while he was sound asleep from the powerful elephant tranquilizer.

Romell Tukes

Chapter 34

Downtown, Chi 'Raq

It was 11:00 p.m. at the dealership, Boss and Kylie were overloaded with a shipment of new cars they had to do inventory for like they had to do at least twice a week. Being that nine employees were mostly college students, Boss and Kylie were the only ones really equipped for handling all the paperwork dealing with the dealership's financial aspect.

Boss was in his office drinking a strong cup of coffee to keep him awake because he had at least two more hours left of paperwork. The past couple of days Boss had been busy with work and trying to stay busy to take his mind off Rosie leaving him.

Since his wife left, he'd been emotionally lost and depressed, but he tried his best to remain strong. He hadn't made time to check his crew, his mom, or his drug spots.

He had a bigger problem going on with someone trying to take over his city, a nigga who was like a ghost to him. Boss was running low on bricks, but Animal told him he was locked up with a nigga in prison who was out and had keys for the low. Boss told Animal to set up a meeting because he needed a plug as fast as possible.

"Kylie, can you find me an insurance policy?" Boss called Kylie on his office phone.

"Yeah, give me a second," she said before hanging up.

Kylie was in her office downstairs with her glasses on, logging all the new cars into the company data which went to D.C. This was a regular night for Kylie. She loved her job and working for Boss was the best part because he treated her like a friend and woman. She had a big crush on him and now with his wife out of the picture, she was enthusiastic about showing him she could be wifey material. She knew if she put her vicious head game on him, she would break him down and make him fall in love.

Kylie spun around in her chair and opened her file cabinet to grab the insurance policy. She looked at the camera monitor real fast but something caught her attention as she saw gunmen dressed in all black running through the car lot toward them.

"Boss, they outside with guns!" Kylie yelled before all the lights went out and the showroom area floor was surrounded by gunmen dressed in all black.

"Boss, they coming upstairs!" she yelled before she got shot in the neck.

Boss busted out of his office with an SK assault rifle shooting the four gunmen creeping upstairs with some snipers in hand.

Bullet swarmed upstairs from below as Boss ducked and ran downstairs where he had more room to maneuver. At the bottom of the stairs, he leaned up against a Lambo as bullets came from everywhere.

Tat! Tat! Tat! Tat! Tat! Tat! Tat! Tat!

Two of the gunmen dropped as Boss hit both shooters with clean headshots. Boss was an elite shooter with any type of gun or rifle it was just a natural gift. Boss saw at least six more shooters, so he fired in their direction while looking at Kylie slumped on the floor. He ran out the exit leading into the parking lot ducking shots coming from behind him.

Boss turned around firing back trying to hold the shooters off because they were on his ass.

Tat! Tat! Tat! Tat! Tat! Tat! Tat!

Boss killed two more shooters as the other four hid behind cars trying not to get caught in the wrath of bullets raining down on them.

As soon as Boss turned around, he felt a sharp pain in his neck. Boss tried to pull the trigger, but his fingers were all numb along with his body. Boss collapsed on the floor, his vision started to fade and he heard a foreign language from the men surrounding him. The gunmen grabbed his body dragging him to a nearby truck. Boss continued to go in and out of consciousness as he heard the familiar language before he blackout from the high dose of elephant tranquilizer.

Chi'Raq Gangstas 2

To Be Continued…
Chi'Raq Gangstas 3
Coming Soon

Submission Guideline

Submit the first three chapters of your completed manuscript to ldpsubmissions@gmail.com, subject line: Your book's title. The manuscript must be in a .doc file and sent as an attachment. Document should be in Times New Roman, double spaced and in size 12 font. Also, provide your synopsis and full contact information. If sending multiple submissions, they must each be in a separate email.

Have a story but no way to send it electronically? You can still submit to LDP/Ca$h Presents. Send in the first three chapters, written or typed, of your completed manuscript to:

LDP: Submissions Dept
Po Box 944
Stockbridge, Ga 30281

DO NOT send original manuscript. Must be a duplicate.

Provide your synopsis and a cover letter containing your full contact information.

Thanks for considering LDP and Ca$h Presents.

Chi'Raq Gangstas 2

Coming Soon from Lock Down Publications/Ca$h Presents

BOW DOWN TO MY GANGSTA

By **Ca$h**

TORN BETWEEN TWO

By **Coffee**

THE STREETS STAINED MY SOUL **II**

By **Marcellus Allen**

BLOOD OF A BOSS **VI**

SHADOWS OF THE GAME II

By **Askari**

LOYAL TO THE GAME **IV**

By **T.J. & Jelissa**

IF LOVING YOU IS WRONG... **III**

By **Jelissa**

TRUE SAVAGE **VIII**

MIDNIGHT CARTEL III

DOPE BOY MAGIC IV

CITY OF KINGZ II

By **Chris Green**

BLAST FOR ME **III**

A SAVAGE DOPEBOY III

CUTTHROAT MAFIA III

DUFFLE BAG CARTEL VI

By **Ghost**

A HUSTLER'S DECEIT III

KILL ZONE **II**

Romell Tukes

By Blakk Diamond

TRAP QUEEN

By Troublesome

YAYO V

GHOST MOB II

Stilloan Robinson

KINGPIN DREAMS III

By Paper Boi Rari

CREAM II

By Yolanda Moore

SON OF A DOPE FIEND III

By Renta

FOREVER GANGSTA II

GLOCKS ON SATIN SHEETS III

By Adrian Dulan

LOYALTY AIN'T PROMISED III

By Keith Williams

THE PRICE YOU PAY FOR LOVE II

By Destiny Skai

I'M NOTHING WITHOUT HIS LOVE II

SINS OF A THUG II

By Monet Dragun

LIFE OF A SAVAGE IV

MURDA SEASON IV

GANGLAND CARTEL III

CHI'RAQ GANGSTAS III

By **Romell Tukes**

QUIET MONEY IV

THUG LIFE II

EXTENDED CLIP II

By **Trai'Quan**

THE STREETS MADE ME III

By **Larry D. Wright**

IF YOU CROSS ME ONCE II

ANGEL III

By **Anthony Fields**

FRIEND OR FOE III

By **Mimi**

SAVAGE STORMS II

By **Meesha**

BLOOD ON THE MONEY III

By J-Blunt

THE STREETS WILL NEVER CLOSE II

By K'ajji

NIGHTMARES OF A HUSTLA III

By King Dream

THE WIFEY I USED TO BE II

By Nicole Goosby

IN THE ARM OF HIS BOSS

By Jamila

MONEY, MURDER & MEMORIES II

Malik D. Rice

CONCRETE KILLAZ II

By Kingpen

HARD AND RUTHLESS II

By Von Wiley Hall

LEVELS TO THIS SHYT II

By Ah'Million

Available Now

RESTRAINING ORDER **I & II**

By **CA$H & Coffee**

LOVE KNOWS NO BOUNDARIES **I II & III**

By **Coffee**

RAISED AS A GOON I, II, III & IV

BRED BY THE SLUMS I, II, III

BLAST FOR ME I & II

ROTTEN TO THE CORE I II III

A BRONX TALE I, II, III

DUFFLE BAG CARTEL I II III IV V

HEARTLESS GOON I II III IV

A SAVAGE DOPEBOY I II

HEARTLESS GOON I II III

DRUG LORDS I II III

CUTTHROAT MAFIA I II

By **Ghost**

LAY IT DOWN **I & II**

LAST OF A DYING BREED I II

BLOOD STAINS OF A SHOTTA I & II III

Romell Tukes

By **Jamaica**

LOYAL TO THE GAME I II III

LIFE OF SIN I, II III

By **TJ & Jelissa**

BLOODY COMMAS I & II

SKI MASK CARTEL I II & III

KING OF NEW YORK I II,III IV V

RISE TO POWER I II III

COKE KINGS I II III IV

BORN HEARTLESS I II III IV

KING OF THE TRAP

By **T.J. Edwards**

IF LOVING HIM IS WRONG…I & II

LOVE ME EVEN WHEN IT HURTS I II III

By **Jelissa**

WHEN THE STREETS CLAP BACK I & II III

THE HEART OF A SAVAGE I II

By **Jibril Williams**

A DISTINGUISHED THUG STOLE MY HEART I II & III

LOVE SHOULDN'T HURT I II III IV

RENEGADE BOYS I II III IV

PAID IN KARMA I II III

SAVAGE STORMS

By **Meesha**

A GANGSTER'S CODE I &, II III

A GANGSTER'S SYN I II III

THE SAVAGE LIFE I II III

CHAINED TO THE STREETS I II III

BLOOD ON THE MONEY I II

By J-Blunt

PUSH IT TO THE LIMIT

By **Bre' Hayes**

BLOOD OF A BOSS **I, II, III, IV, V**

SHADOWS OF THE GAME

By **Askari**

THE STREETS BLEED MURDER **I, II & III**

THE HEART OF A GANGSTA I II& III

By **Jerry Jackson**

CUM FOR ME I II III IV V VI

An **LDP Erotica Collaboration**

BRIDE OF A HUSTLA **I II & II**

THE FETTI GIRLS **I, II& III**

CORRUPTED BY A GANGSTA I, II III, IV

BLINDED BY HIS LOVE

THE PRICE YOU PAY FOR LOVE

DOPE GIRL MAGIC I II III

By **Destiny Skai**

WHEN A GOOD GIRL GOES BAD

By **Adrienne**

THE COST OF LOYALTY I II III

By Kweli

A GANGSTER'S REVENGE **I II III & IV**

THE BOSS MAN'S DAUGHTERS I II III IV V

A SAVAGE LOVE **I & II**

BAE BELONGS TO ME I II

A HUSTLER'S DECEIT I, II, III

WHAT BAD BITCHES DO I, II, III

SOUL OF A MONSTER I II III

KILL ZONE

A DOPE BOY'S QUEEN I II

By **Aryanna**

A KINGPIN'S AMBITON

A KINGPIN'S AMBITION **II**

I MURDER FOR THE DOUGH

By **Ambitious**

TRUE SAVAGE I II III IV V VI VII

DOPE BOY MAGIC I, II, III

MIDNIGHT CARTEL I II

CITY OF KINGZ

By **Chris Green**

A DOPEBOY'S PRAYER

By **Eddie "Wolf" Lee**

THE KING CARTEL **I, II & III**

By **Frank Gresham**

THESE NIGGAS AIN'T LOYAL **I, II & III**

By **Nikki Tee**

GANGSTA SHYT **I II &III**

By **CATO**

THE ULTIMATE BETRAYAL

By **Phoenix**

BOSS'N UP **I , II & III**

By **Royal Nicole**
I LOVE YOU TO DEATH
By Destiny J
I RIDE FOR MY HITTA
I STILL RIDE FOR MY HITTA
By **Misty Holt**
LOVE & CHASIN' PAPER
By **Qay Crockett**
TO DIE IN VAIN
SINS OF A HUSTLA
By **ASAD**
BROOKLYN HUSTLAZ
By **Boogsy Morina**
BROOKLYN ON LOCK I & II
By **Sonovia**
GANGSTA CITY
By **Teddy Duke**
A DRUG KING AND HIS DIAMOND I & II III
A DOPEMAN'S RICHES
HER MAN, MINE'S TOO I, II
CASH MONEY HO'S
THE WIFEY I USED TO BE
By Nicole Goosby
TRAPHOUSE KING **I II & III**
KINGPIN KILLAZ I II III
STREET KINGS I II
PAID IN BLOOD **I II**

Romell Tukes

CARTEL KILLAZ I II III

DOPE GODS I II

By **Hood Rich**

LIPSTICK KILLAH **I, II, III**

CRIME OF PASSION I II & III

FRIEND OR FOE I II

By **Mimi**

STEADY MOBBN' **I, II, III**

THE STREETS STAINED MY SOUL

By **Marcellus Allen**

WHO SHOT YA **I, II, III**

SON OF A DOPE FIEND I II

Renta

GORILLAZ IN THE BAY **I II III IV**

TEARS OF A GANGSTA I II

3X KRAZY I II

DE'KARI

TRIGGADALE I II III

Elijah R. Freeman

GOD BLESS THE TRAPPERS I, II, III

THESE SCANDALOUS STREETS I, II, III

FEAR MY GANGSTA I, II, III IV, V

THESE STREETS DON'T LOVE NOBODY I, II

BURY ME A G I, II, III, IV, V

A GANGSTA'S EMPIRE I, II, III, IV

THE DOPEMAN'S BODYGAURD I II

THE REALEST KILLAZ I II III

Chi'Raq Gangstas 2

Tranay Adams
THE STREETS ARE CALLING
Duquie Wilson
MARRIED TO A BOSS... I II III
By Destiny Skai & Chris Green
KINGZ OF THE GAME I II III IV V
Playa Ray
SLAUGHTER GANG I II III
RUTHLESS HEART I II III
By Willie Slaughter
FUK SHYT
By Blakk Diamond
DON'T F#CK WITH MY HEART I II
By Linnea
ADDICTED TO THE DRAMA I II III
IN THE ARM OF HIS BOSS II
By Jamila
YAYO I II III IV
A SHOOTER'S AMBITION I II
By S. Allen
TRAP GOD I II III
By Troublesome
FOREVER GANGSTA
GLOCKS ON SATIN SHEETS I II
By Adrian Dulan
TOE TAGZ I II III
LEVELS TO THIS SHYT

Romell Tukes

By Ah'Million
KINGPIN DREAMS I II
By Paper Boi Rari
CONFESSIONS OF A GANGSTA I II III
By Nicholas Lock
I'M NOTHING WITHOUT HIS LOVE
SINS OF A THUG
By Monet Dragun
CAUGHT UP IN THE LIFE I II III
By Robert Baptiste
NEW TO MONEY, MURDER & MEMORIES
THE GAME I II III
By **Malik D. Rice**
LIFE OF A SAVAGE I II III
A GANGSTA'S QUR'AN I II III
MURDA SEASON I II III
GANGLAND CARTEL I II
CHI'RAQ GANGSTAS I II
By **Romell Tukes**
LOYALTY AIN'T PROMISED I II
By Keith Williams
QUIET MONEY I II III
THUG LIFE
EXTENDED CLIP
By **Trai'Quan**
THE STREETS MADE ME I II
By **Larry D. Wright**

210

THE ULTIMATE SACRIFICE I, II, III, IV, V, VI
KHADIFI
IF YOU CROSS ME ONCE
ANGEL I II
By **Anthony Fields**
THE LIFE OF A HOOD STAR
By Ca$h & Rashia Wilson
THE STREETS WILL NEVER CLOSE
By K'ajji
CREAM
By Yolanda Moore
NIGHTMARES OF A HUSTLA I II
By King Dream
CONCRETE KILLAZ
By Kingpen
HARD AND RUTHLESS
By Von Wiley Hall
GHOST MOB II
Stilloan Robinson

<u>BOOKS BY LDP'S CEO, CA$H</u>

<u>TRUST IN NO MAN</u>

<u>TRUST IN NO MAN 2</u>

<u>TRUST IN NO MAN 3</u>

<u>BONDED BY BLOOD</u>

<u>SHORTY GOT A THUG</u>

<u>THUGS CRY</u>

<u>THUGS CRY 2</u>

<u>THUGS CRY 3</u>

<u>TRUST NO BITCH</u>

<u>TRUST NO BITCH 2</u>

<u>TRUST NO BITCH 3</u>

<u>TIL MY CASKET DROPS</u>

<u>RESTRAINING ORDER</u>

<u>RESTRAINING ORDER 2</u>

<u>IN LOVE WITH A CONVICT</u>

<u>LIFE OF A HOOD STAR</u>

Chi'Raq Gangstas 2

CPSIA information can be obtained
at www.ICGtesting.com
Printed in the USA
LVHW051326140321
681503LV00007B/249